D1685177

SURVIVAL INSTINCT

Ever since Lucy's childhood sweet-heart dropped a bombshell and left her coping single-handed, she's been in survival mode. Then handsome incomer Rupert arrives with cute ducks, amazing culinary skills and a lifestyle country vet Lucy always dreamed of. But someone is lying to her, and it could be him. Lucy must rely on her instincts to choose who to trust. And if that's Rupert, will he finally share his deepest secrets and let her into his heart?

SUE COOK

SURVIVAL INSTINCT

Complete and Unabridged

LINFORD
Leicester

First published in Great Britain in 2022 by
D.C. Thomson & Co. Ltd.
Dundee

First Linford Edition
published 2025
by arrangement with
the author and
D.C. Thomson & Co. Ltd.
Dundee

*A catalogue record for this book is available
from the British Library.*

ISBN 978–1–4448–5467–1

Published by
Ulverscroft Limited
Anstey, Leicestershire

Printed and bound by CPI Group (UK) Ltd., Croydon, CR0 4YY

This book is printed on acid-free paper

Village Newcomer

Lucy Pugh closed Attila the rabbit's notes and sank her head on to her arms. Five minutes, that's all she needed. A power nap and she'd be . . .

Her phone pinged once, twice, to announce incoming texts and her computer hooted with an important message.

'Fishcakes,' she muttered and straightened up just as the door of her room burst open.

'Don't bother with that visit.' Elaine, her practice manager, strode in, one hand pointing at the computer. 'I told the receptionist to pass it to the vets in Bickerston. You need to go home and rest.'

Lucy looked at the screen and frowned.

'Longmeadow. That place has been empty for years. Has someone bought it?'

She clicked on the visit request for *ducks acting oddly*. The name linked to the request was unfamiliar.

'Rupert Cheating,' Elaine told her.

Lucy pointed at the screen.

'It says Chetwynd here.'

Elaine rolled her eyes.

'He pronounces it 'Cheating', apparently. Sounds like another of those posh types with more money than sense. We've seen a few of those over the years, haven't we?'

They had. Lucy made a snap decision.

'I'll go. Ducks are notorious for behaving normally until seriously ill and I'm the only vet for miles with an interest in birds.

'Besides,' she added with a grin, 'I always wanted to look around that place.'

'Didn't you and Jamie think of buying it?'

Lucy nodded. For as long as she could remember she'd coveted the idyllic smallholding. Longmeadow offered the perfect compromise between working full time as a vet and owning a farm like the one she'd grown up on.

When it had come up for sale her ex had, probably sensibly, forbidden her to view it.

'It was a pipedream. The asking price was way outside our budget. I dread to think where I'd be now if I was paying a mortgage on something that size.'

Elaine's lips tightened and Lucy waited for a tirade against her ex-fiancé, Jamie.

She busied herself by checking her phone and saw the avatar of best friend, Michael, proud in the yellow jacket and peaked cap of his special constable uniform.

The sight cheered Lucy up. His message was less positive, however.

She turned to Elaine.

'There's been another theft!'

Elaine nodded.

'I know, Jack Turner's young stallion. Cheeky so-and-sos! Whoever's behind this is getting bolder. That's the biggest animal yet to go missing.'

'Jack Turner,' Lucy mused. 'Isn't his farm near Longmeadow House, where the request for a home visit came from?'

Why was she even asking? She'd lived

in North Millton all her life and knew every farm within five miles.

Elaine put her hands on her hips.

'You're going on that visit, aren't you?'

Lucy smiled brightly and dropped her phone into her bag.

'If Mr Chetwynd has enough money to buy Longmeadow he'll have enough to pay his vet bills.'

Since the practice finances caused her manager even more consternation than Lucy's heavy workload she figured Elaine wouldn't have an answer to that.

'Unless he's spent it all on that house!'

Touché, Elaine.

'There's only one way to find out.' Lucy gulped the last of her coffee, then stood. 'I promise I'll go home for a nap afterwards.'

Elaine shook her head and exited, leaving Lucy to ponder the newcomer. Rupert Chetwynd-pronounced-Cheating did suggest a privileged type who wanted to live closer to the land without understanding how hard that was.

Lucy didn't mind unless the animals suffered through ignorance. Sadly, she'd seen that happen. Hopefully these ducks were healthy and their owner was being overcautious.

The words of Tony Holden, her old senior partner, came to her.

'Half the diagnosis and management lies in knowing the owner.'

Lucy knew nothing about this new-comer. It was time to consult the village oracle.

Josie, the Oracle

Leaving the building Lucy strode along the pavement and around the corner on to the high street, where Josie Grainger had revolutionised the village shop by turning it into a community store and post office.

The shop had been dying and faced closing once and for all, but Josie had had vision. She'd bought the premises next door and turned both into a grocer's that people came to before the small superstore on the outskirts of Bickerston, the market town about five miles from North Millton.

Lucy pushed open the door to the tinkle of a traditional bell. Inside lay a mouthwatering display: homemade sandwiches; local organic milk in returnable bottles; a refill station for dry goods such as lentils and oats; fresh free-range eggs in a basket lined with straw and artisan sourdoughs stacked on a sloping wooden rack.

The shop also carried staples like sliced loaves, tinned tomatoes and tubs of salt.

Walking inside always lifted Lucy's spirits. Here, in this small corner of Lancashire, the world was travelling in the right direction.

Josie completed this comforting image with plump pink cheeks and a cheery smile, reminiscent of the sort of mum who has a plate of chocolate biscuits permanently ready for unexpected visitors.

Lucy was the only customer. She picked up a pack of egg and mayo sandwiches and took it to the counter.

'Morning, Luce.' Josie took the pack and waved it at the scanner.

Lucy estimated the postmistress was 20 years older than her and 10 times perkier. Modern, horn-rimmed glasses and a few ash-blonde strands escaping from her bun completed the young-at-heart look.

'No time to make your own lunch again?' Josie continued. 'Not surprised — you look shattered. Been up half the night, I hear, with horse colic on the other side of Bickerston. They can be tricky, can't they?'

As Lucy had long since stopped trying to understand how Josie heard everything she didn't ask the origin of this information.

She concentrated instead on diverting Josie into a more useful direction.

'Yes, I passed Longmeadow House. The 'For Sale' sign has gone.'

'Oh, Lucy, love, you are way behind the news. The new owner moved in two months back!' Josie answered instantly. 'One of those well-to-do names that's said differently from how it's spelled. From down south.

'Worked in the City, I heard. Retired early and has gone organic.

'He must be loaded if he can retire at his age and buy Esme Wilberforce's old place! He's only in his mid-thirties, I should say, but he has some odd ideas.

'Self-sufficiency or something. Apparently, the animals are going to fend for themselves because he won't buy in food.'

With a growing sense of unease Lucy listened as Josie counted out her change.

'We've come across a few of those before, haven't we?' Josie continued. 'He won't last long once he realises it's not all designer wellies and waving fields of corn on a sunny summer afternoon!

'A couple of awkward lambings in the middle of the night, a month of rain when he wants to cut hay and he'll be wishing he'd never heard o' Lancashire!

'Let's hope it's not a repeat of that football player with the pigs,' she finished with a sniff.

'Yes.' Lucy shuddered.

The consequences of that disastrous venture still made her blood boil.

'Anyway, he's single.' Josie opened her eyes wide in a 'take note' gesture.

'Who?'

'Him at Longmeadow. Long dark hair, brown eyes. Wears a shirt like a model.

'He's living in that enormous house all by himself. Why not drop round to give him a few tips?' Josie suggested with an exaggerated wink.

Lucy pocketed her change, picked up the sandwiches and turned to go.

'No, thanks, Josie. Not after you-know-who.'

At the same time Lucy was suspecting she might have to give this newcomer a stern lecture. If Rupert Chetwynd didn't feed his ducks they would quickly sicken or leave.

'Talking of Jamie . . .' Josie changed tack effortlessly. 'I hear he's starting a Master's course. Something to do with crocodiles, I believe.'

'Reproduction in amphibious reptiles of the Florida Everglades,' Lucy corrected, if only to prove Josie wasn't the only one with privileged information. 'Alligators, not crocodiles.'

And good luck to him, she added to herself gleefully, out there in all that steamy heat, surrounded by sneaky predators with long rows of vicious teeth.

'Still, with all that lovely sunshine, aren't you tempted? He asked you to go with him, didn't he?'

'Not listening,' Lucy threw back over

her shoulder as she turned to leave.

Yes, her ex had generously suggested she should accompany him as he pursued his preferred career — the life goal he'd kept hidden from everyone, including Lucy, until Tony, his father, had died.

But she had made her choice and her dream won out over his every time.

Despite everything she would not admit defeat and run after him, even if that would mean living in the sunshine state and swapping endless nights on call for sunbathing by a pool.

Besides, it was too late now. According to his mother Jamie was in a new relationship with a marine biologist.

He'd moved on and that was what Lucy was trying to do, too.

Josie's voice followed her out of the little shop.

'Make sure you call on him at Longmeadow House. He's as fit as Joe Wicks but ten times better looking, they say.

'Pecs to die for and abs you could roll pastry on. Eyes like . . .'

Lucy strode confidently on.

'Still not listening!'

After Jamie, Lucy would never trust a man again.

Permaculture

Longmeadow House was a long, low, stone building. In the valley bottom a wide, shallow river babbled over pale stones.

On either side verdant pastures trimmed with neat stone walls clothed the gentle lower slopes of the western Pennines, giving way to darker woodland that straddled the hilltops.

Since moving in Rupert Chetwynd had risen with the sun every morning and thought he'd moved to heaven. True, the house needed work, but decorating used up as many calories as a gym workout.

He needed to pay for double-glazing, too, but the setting couldn't be prettier and cycling here was far safer than in London.

The only threat to this Nirvana lay shivering in the old stables.

'Alison, sweetheart, what's wrong?'

The grey Indian runner duck sat in the corner of a stall with her bill tucked under her wing and her feathers fluffed up.

She reminded him of himself the last time he'd caught flu.

'I wish you could talk. I wish you could tell me what's wrong and how I could put it right.'

'And I hope the vet arrives soon,' he added, glancing at his watch.

He didn't expect much from the vet but at least he'd share his concern with an expert.

'Hello?'

A woman's voice. Rupert straightened up from his crouched position.

'She's here, Alison. Help is on its way.'

He strode to the stables door and leaned out.

'Are you the vet?'

About his age, the woman with shoulder-length, light brown hair held back by a practical Alice band would be pretty if she weren't so obviously tired.

Pallid skin and dull, sunken eyes suggested sleepless nights. A too-big waxed jacket hung from her shoulders and her cheekbones were too sharp.

Someone, he judged, wasn't looking after themselves.

'Yes, Lucy Pugh. Are you . . . ?'

'Rupert Chetwynd,' he supplied.

He had concluded years ago it was quicker to offer his name than to correct people when they pronounced it as it looked.

'Thank you for coming out. Yesterday the whole flock seemed lethargic. But now, well, see for yourself. Alison is in here.'

He returned to the gloomy interior of the stables and the vet joined him.

'Alison?' she asked.

Rupert pointed to the duck.

'You'll think me sentimental but her feathers are the same salt and pepper colour as my auntie Alison's hair.'

Whatever Lucy Pugh thought she hid it well. Her eyes rested briefly on the bird before flitting around the rest of the stall that served as the ducks' sleeping area.

Despite being tired she was alert and, he suspected, shrewd. Rupert tried to examine the stall with objective eyes, too.

He'd adapted it to keep the ducks safe and comfortable at night — fresh wood shavings on the floor; a water bowl; a sluice channel beyond the door he'd fashioned to contain them.

He spotted nothing amiss.

When she had finished her visual check the vet returned her attention to him.

'You're worried about the whole flock?'

Rupert dragged his thoughts away from the unusual smoky-grey colour of Lucy Pugh's eyes They would light up her face if only they sparkled.

'Yes. I got them four days ago. Eight ducks and a drake.'

She nodded. In approval or to encourage him? Her frosty exterior suggested he was on trial and it spurred him on to prove he knew what he was doing.

'They seemed fine initially, though very nervous of me, naturally. Then, yesterday, they hardly moved from bushes near their pond and barely touched their food.'

16

He thought he detected a flicker of surprise cross her face.

'This morning,' he continued, placing his hand on the door to the stall, 'Alison didn't run out with the others.'

'Show me the food,' she demanded.

He led her to a metal bin where he stored the sack of proprietary pellets.

'I made sure it's duck-friendly. Antibiotics in some poultry feed can poison ducks, can't they?'

Lucy checked the contents.

'Yes. That's a common mistake. Do you have much experience with poultry?'

So she suspected the illness might be his fault? Rupert straightened.

'I've never kept them before, if that's what you mean, but I've been on an animal husbandry course. When I do something I do it well.

'Animals are integral to the success of permaculture. Giving my animals the best life imaginable is paramount.'

Lucy looked at him with puzzlement.

'Permaculture? What's that?'

Here Rupert was on familiar ground.

Permaculture was his new life.

Care for people, care for the earth and take only his fair share from it — these were his new mantras and he was determined to stick by them.

He would help safeguard the world for other people's children.

'It's short for permanent agriculture,' he explained. 'A system of living as sustainably as possible.'

'You mean organic farming?'

Rupert nodded.

'Yes, but more than that.' He took a deep breath, ready to begin a more detailed description, but Lucy interrupted.

'It sounds great. Can I see the pond where you keep the others?'

'What? Oh, yes.' Rupert snapped back to the current problem.

Lucy Pugh seemed abrupt, which was acceptable if she was also competent. Anyway, he was used to this reaction by now.

An incomer, they called him — someone new to the area. Most of the folk he had encountered so far were polite but wary of him.

He'd have to earn his place in the community.

A Spate of Thefts

Rupert led Lucy out of the stable block and through a gate in a hedge. In the field beyond his other ducks lay at the edge of a natural pond.

His step faltered as they didn't respond by looking up and 'parping', as he called it. While Indian runner ducks did quack sometimes he'd quickly learned that, more often, they gave quieter 'parps' or muttered to themselves.

'Oh, no. Don't tell me they're all sick! I couldn't bear it.'

'Let's not jump to conclusions.'

Lucy led the way towards the little group. Eight heads shot up and eight pairs of eyes fixed on the humans. Suddenly they leaped up, parped and ran to the far side of the pond.

Relief flooded through Rupert. His shoulders, that had been up round his ears, dropped and relaxed.

'They seem fine.' Lucy said what he was thinking. 'But I want to check for poisonous plants.'

She headed towards a wild area in the far corner, a semi-thicket of brambles, dandelions and long grass where the flock had spent yesterday hiding.

He strode after her.

'I checked but I only found a few buttercups. That shouldn't hurt, should it?'

Lucy kept a few paces ahead, sharp eyes darting this way and that.

'As you say, just a few buttercups. Not enough to cause a problem.'

Rupert let out an enormous sigh.

'Thank you. Going on a course is one thing but when you suddenly own real, living creatures it all seems a lot more uncertain somehow.'

A hand rested on his arm. He looked down into her earnest eyes.

'You're doing fine and your ducks have a great home. I suspect an infection which they may have caught before you bought them. Shall we examine Alison now?'

She smiled and Rupert's heart kicked. He told himself it was nothing to do with physical attraction, but her reassurance that he had not caused Alison's illness.

That warmth spreading deep in his core was relief, not connection.

'Focus on the ducks,' he told himself as he returned the smile nervously. 'This vet is comforting a client with sick animals. It's nothing personal.'

He couldn't let it be personal. Romance was off his radar for the foreseeable future, as was marriage and starting a family.

He had other priorities now.

Despite being sick Alison took some catching. Eventually he had her firmly but gently encased in his arms.

He murmured reassurance as he carried her to a workbench with more light.

Lucy Pugh examined the duck with speed and efficiency. Rupert saw he could have faith in her. Finally she replaced her stethoscope in her bag.

'As I thought. Probably a lung infection.'

'Is it serious?'

'Potentially. I'll take Alison to the

surgery, run some tests and start treatment.'

'What about the others?'

Would they sicken one by one? The idea nauseated him. How could he own animals for such a short length before losing them?

Lucy smiled reassuringly again.

'Just keep an eye on them.'

She must have sensed his worries because she put her hand on his arm again.

'Really, you're doing fine. Animals get sick just like humans, no matter how much care you take.'

His heart skipped. He'd been right — she was attractive. Her words calmed him but he also felt that connection again.

He reminded himself she was just doing her job.

'Thanks. That means a lot.'

Lucy led the way back towards the car.

'I heard your animals would have to fend for themselves,' she said over her shoulder. Rupert gritted his teeth and followed with Alison. The locals had been gossiping, then.

'Commercial poultry feed contains environment-damaging components such as soya beans that are shipped halfway across the world,' he explained. 'I hope to do without them eventually but I need to develop local sources of well-balanced foodstuffs first.'

'Good luck with that.'

From her tone he deduced she categorised him as mad as a box of frogs. Never mind. He'd show everyone.

'Farming is a hard life,' she continued. 'Ideals are all very well but you'll be working all day, all year round. If you have no-one to share the load it can break you.'

Rupert saw her gaze flick to the house. She was wondering if he was married or had a family. He forced the knot of pain down deep inside him.

'I live alone,' he said, 'but don't worry. I'm used to hard work and long hours.'

Her soft lips thinned into a grim line.

'I expect you're used to holidays as

well. Unless you can arrange for someone to care for the livestock you can forget those.'

He had thought about that. It was a sacrifice he was willing to make for now.

He knew there would come a time when he would need a break and he hoped, by then, he would have built up sufficient links within the community to have people look after his few animals while he was away.

He looked across the valley, at patches of sunlight scampering across the fields.

'Why would I want to leave somewhere as beautiful as this?'

Lucy laughed.

'Just wait till winter!'

They'd arrived back at the cars. A red car had joined his and Lucy's and a police officer stood beside it. He was tall and lean.

'Hello, Michael,' Lucy said as she opened the boot of her silver Subaru. 'What are you doing here?'

'I could ask you the same thing.'

'Alison is sick.'

Michael raised his eyebrows.

'Alison?'

Lucy pointed as Rupert placed the duck carefully into the cage she carried in her boot.

'It's a duck,' Michael said.

It appeared he was not sentimental about animals.

Lucy turned to Rupert.

'Michael and I went to school together. He's a special constable now with the rural crimes squad.'

Rupert frowned.

'Have I done something wrong?'

Michael shook his head.

'I came to ask if you saw anything suspicious last night. Uncle Fester disappeared from that field, just over the way.' He pointed across the valley.

Rupert stared at him.

'Uncle Fester?'

'Jack Turner's horse,' Lucy explained. 'Your neighbour who owns the land on the other side of the valley.'

Ah, yes. Rupert had met Jack soon after moving in. An older guy with a neat goatee had called round to introduce himself.

Occasionally they'd pass in their cars and exchange waves.

'This area has suffered a spate of small animal thefts,' Michael continued.

Rupert didn't understand.

'A horse doesn't sound small.'

'I mean small numbers. A sheep here, a pair of piglets there. It would make more sense if entire flocks vanished.'

Rupert looked across the valley.

'There was a horse there yesterday. I don't see it now.'

'Yup, that was Uncle Fester. Anyway, it's good to see Longmeadow occupied again,' Michael said. 'It's been empty five years.

'Didn't you look at it once?' he asked Lucy who turned away.

'It was way out of our price bracket.'

Michael's eyes followed Lucy to the driver's door. Rupert saw longing there: the officer was in love.

But did she return those feelings? Presumably not, if she'd looked at

Longmeadow with a partner.

This was good for Rupert as there was no risk of the two of them becoming involved and it all ending in tears.

As Lucy's car disappeared from view the other man looked at Rupert.

'So, did you notice anything unusual last night? A horsebox? Odd noises?'

Rupert shook his head.

'I flake out at nine and am unconscious until the sun wakes me. I didn't even notice the horse had gone. Sorry.'

Michael left his card in case Rupert remembered something later. He also left a warning to secure his property.

Rupert looked at the simple latch that fastened the stables door and bit his lip.

He thought he'd left that sort of thing behind in London.

Just Friends

Today Alison lay like a safety barrier on the examination table between her handsome owner and Lucy.

'Fortunately it's not the fungal infection I suspected,' Lucy explained, looking anywhere but into Rupert's rich brown eyes.

Even so she struggled to find an area that didn't set her pulse racing. He was tanned and toned, his loose-fitting T-shirt doing little to hide his lean yet muscular build.

His jaw-length, untamed, dark hair reminded her of a carefree surfer's and his smile was as warm as the sun.

Lucy struggled to keep her attention on the medical problem — Alison.

'I'm still awaiting lab results but I'm sure it's a straightforward infection. How are the others?'

'All fine. Seven ducks a-laying. And eating me out of house and home!'

His grin made heat rise in her cheeks.

She turned away.

'I've started her on antibiotics. Give them twice a day for a week and don't eat her eggs for two weeks.'

'How do I give her the medicine?' Rupert no longer looked confident.

She picked up a dummy syringe and turned back to him, keeping her eyes on Alison.

'Like this.'

She demonstrated how to open the bill by pressing where it hinged.

'Deliver the medicine into the throat thus. It's easier with two people,' she added, 'when you've not done it before.'

'But one person can do it,' he pointed out. 'What about the other ducks?'

Lucy shook her head.

'If they're well just monitor them. They were probably stressed, then Alison picked up a virus or something. That happens to birds as well as humans.'

Rupert nodded.

'Collect the medicine from Reception and I'll phone you when the results are back.' Lucy dismissed him with a polite smile.

After he'd gone she threw herself into cleaning the examination table, to banish all thoughts of Rupert's fine physique — standing with his wide shoulders back, his broad chest out.

Finally, her cheeks warm through effort and not discomposure, she sat in front of the computer with a cup of herbal tea.

She had actually asked for coffee but Elaine had said that would prevent a good night's sleep. Instead she had brought something tinged green.

A little paperwork remained before Lucy could go home. She'd sling a frozen pizza in the oven and get an early night.

Maybe she'd even pick up a bag of ready-made salad from Josie's.

Before she left Michael arrived. They met in the coffee room where he made himself herbal tea, too.

'If you made a coffee I could have one without Elaine knowing,' Lucy suggested hopefully.

He shook his head.

'You know I only have one cup of caffeine a day. You should, too.'

Lucy sighed.

'I envy your self-control. What's for tea tonight? Seaweed?'

He scowled.

'I'm having a rare steak with spinach and sweet potato. A balance of lean protein and vegetables crammed with micro-nutrients. Unlike you, I value what I put into my body.'

'It's not that I don't value it, I just don't have time,' Lucy explained.

Michael was looking great on his healthy diet — lean and fit, every inch the endurance athlete.

He looked at her accusingly.

'You look beat. How's the search for another vet going? Any takers?'

Lucy sagged.

'A few enquiries. There's a student due to graduate this summer who sounds keen but they won't be fully qualified for some months yet.'

She pressed her fingers to her eyes.

'If he doesn't join I'm not sure how long I can go on, Michael.'

'Come here.'

He put down the mug he'd been stirring and gathered her into an awkward embrace. His body felt hard and bony.

Lucy found herself mentally comparing it to a hug from Rupert. Not that she'd ever received one.

Or ever would. That would not happen.

'I'm here for you, you know that,' Michael continued.

Yes, Lucy could rely on him. He'd been the one constant apart from her family these last 12 months.

But she couldn't relax in his arms. She suspected he harboured feelings she could never reciprocate so it would be wrong to encourage him.

She pulled away slightly and he released her.

'You're a good friend, Michael, but there's only so much you can do.'

He picked up his mug again but kept his gaze on her.

'You need to move on, Lucy. Forget the past. Jamie lied to everyone, not just you.

'He kept what he really wanted deep inside him because he would never upset his father.

'Not everyone is like that. I'm not like that.'

She managed a weak smile.

'I know, but you can't give me back my ability to trust.'

'Perhaps not but I can take you out to dinner,' he said hopefully. 'When did you last eat anything with vitamins?'

Lucy thought about the egg sandwich. Eggs contained B12.

'Yesterday,' she said, even though Michael was talking about eating the rainbow. 'I'll pass on dinner — I need an early night again.

'I won't be good company. And you have steak waiting for you.'

He sighed and fished the tea bag out of his drink.

'You need a new life, Lucy.'

'Things will improve — they have to.

If this practice fails I'll have to move away to find another job.'

Lucy was talking to herself now, speaking aloud her constant fears.

'I've always lived in North Millton. I love it here and I love the people. All I ever wanted to do was be their vet. How can I live somewhere else?'

Michael looked at her for a long time, his mouth formed into a thoughtful pucker.

She knew he was wondering about challenging her.

'Anyway.' He suddenly became animated again and blew on his drink. 'I came to ask you about the duck chap from Longmeadow.'

'Rupert Chetwynd?'

Michael nodded and sipped.

'You seemed friendly.'

'I only met him yesterday.'

'So you know nothing about him?'

Apart from his carefree hair, his love for animals, his dedication to safeguarding the environment, his face that she couldn't shake from her head and strong but gentle arms she suspected she'd feel safe in?

'No. Josie Grainger thinks he worked in London. Why?'

'Just that the animal thefts started shortly after he arrived.'

Lucy stared at him.

'You don't suspect him, do you?'

'Not really, but these thefts are odd and we have no leads.'

'Where would he put Uncle Fester? I didn't see a horse at Longmeadow. Did you?' she argued.

Michael shrugged.

'I didn't look. What about you?'

'No, but I wasn't expecting a horse.'

She cast her mind back to the visit to Longmeadow and ran through the scene as she remembered it.

'He has old stables but apart from his ducks and a workbench they were empty.

'I don't think he'd be that stupid,' she reasoned aloud. 'He seems too altruistic. I can't see a back-to-the-country-let's-save-the-planet type taking other people's livestock, can you? Unless it was to save them from the chop.'

'You're probably right. But keep your eyes and ears open, will you? Because we desperately need a break.'

★ ★ ★

When the last few results returned from the lab Lucy picked up the phone and rang Rupert with the good news.

'How is Alison?'

'Back to normal but my nerves are shot! Getting her to open her bill appeared simple when you did it. When I try I'm wrestling a crazed beast!'

Lucy laughed.

'And the others?'

'Eggs off every one — except the drake!'

Lucy did some sums. Eight eggs a day added up to fifty-six a week, forty-nine if you excluded Alison's which he needed to discard for now.

'What will you do with all those eggs?'

'Sell them. I need an income.'

'I thought you were rich,' she said

before her internal censor stopped her.

'Whoever told you that was wrong,' he replied without offence. 'I'm a working man; always have been.

'I'll be at the farmer's market in Bickerston on Saturday, selling my produce. Will I see you there?'

Lucy felt wistful. She often meant to visit the fortnightly market but rarely succeeded. If she wasn't on call, she was sleeping or tackling the backlog of housework.

There was her dad to visit, too. They only had each other now. Locally, anyway. Her sister had emigrated to Canada.

This weekend was technically free and it would be good to do something different. It would also support small businesses in their community, something she felt passionate about.

Community lay at the heart of rural living.

'Maybe,' she said.

'Great! I'll watch out for you.'

The Missing Cyclist

As Lucy ended the call with Rupert, Elaine entered with her electronic notebook.

'We need to talk about money.'

Lucy put her head in her hands.

'As long as you tell me we have some!'

Elaine described income and outgoings for the month.

'Unless some of your debtors cough up, the staff wages will push the current account past your overdraft limit. That puts your interest payment at risk which risks defaulting on the loan. Which —'

Lucy put a hand up to halt the flow.

'Which means the bank will demand payment. I'll have to sell my third of the premises and Jamie and his mum will buy me out.'

This perilous state was not of her doing. Just over a year ago the practice had reduced from three partners to one, lumbering Lucy with a mortgage on the recently built practice extension as well as the home she once shared with Jamie.

The job she'd dreamed of since child-hood and the life in the community she called home were under threat.

'I don't suppose you won the lottery?'

Lucy gave Elaine a look. In her opin-ion buying a lottery ticket was as good as throwing your money into the gutter.

'How about getting a lodger?' Elaine tried next.

Lucy slumped lower in her chair.

'Have you been talking to my father?'

He wanted her to let out her house and move back in with him, which was as close to admitting failure as selling up.

Lucy's house was her refuge, some-where to retreat. If she relinquished that she might as well relinquish everything.

She wasn't ready for that. There was fight left in her no matter how dark the outlook.

'OK.' Elaine frowned. 'How about renting the spare room off Reception to a pet psychologist?'

'You've been watching too much day-time TV,' Lucy commented.

'Honestly, it's very popular. How many pets do you see with behavioural issues?'

Quite a few, Lucy thought, but said nothing. Instead, she pulled the notebook screen closer.

'Let's see who owes us what.'

Her despair deepened as she read the list of familiar names. It included Jack Turner, Uncle Fester's owner, who owed almost as much as the rest put together.

Elaine had sent him several reminders including a stiff final warning. The next step was the small claims court. But Lucy didn't have the heart to do that immediately after him losing Uncle Fester.

Many farmers were struggling financially without valuable animals disappearing.

'Hopefully Jack's insurance company will pay out soon,' she prayed aloud.

Elaine tutted.

'Don't hold your breath. That man's as tight as a rusty screw. Tony always said Jack Turner treated the practice as a free loan.'

'Oh? How did Tony get him to settle up?'

'It would reach the point where he refused to visit unless Jack paid. Jack knew Tony was the only decent horse vet for miles.'

Would Jack pay up if Lucy refused to visit? Tony had been a horse specialist. Jack may no longer have the same loyalty and shift his custom to the vets in Bickerston.

If that happened, though, he wouldn't be racking up more debt with her.

She took the list home with her and perused it over a glass of wine while waiting for yet another pizza to cook.

Her phone pinged with a text from Michael. Two geese had disappeared from a rescue centre and a Tamworth boar had been taken from a farm.

Michael didn't have to ask her to stay alert for the relevant animals in case someone brought them in for attention — that had become second nature.

Lucy added the geese — which she realised she had treated in the past —

and boar to the growing list that included Uncle Fester.

So far she had seen none of the missing animals.

Either they'd been sent for meat or sold out of the area. Still, Michael wouldn't be doing his job if he didn't circulate the details.

Lucy didn't make it to the farmer's market and Rupert's stall. She spent Saturday shopping at the discount supermarket in Bickerston instead and catching up on washing and ironing.

This triggered guilt that she couldn't exactly explain. She hardly knew Rupert and had made no promises, after all.

Alison's 'dad' was just another client. A very attractive client, of course, but that was why she needed to stay away — absence would reduce temptation.

The problem was, Rupert was also an incomer who would need a lot of support if he were to make a success of Longmeadow by himself.

Lucy wanted to support someone who obviously loved animals as much as she

43

did and whose heart seemed in the right place.

But what would happen to her own heart if she got too close?

No, Rupert had made his bed and must lie in it without her, metaphorically speaking.

She'd provide professional advice as and when needed, but no more.

★ ★ ★

The weeks dragged on in the same round of disturbed nights, long days and still no definite takers for the vacant vet's post at the practice.

One Monday evening Lucy was finally heading home after a call out right at the end of surgery.

The owner bred boxer dogs and had asked Lucy to attend an experienced mum whose labour had stopped after delivering only two puppies.

She spent an hour helping to deliver the rest of the litter. Finally, with a last rub of mum's head and a smile at eight healthy, wriggling pups, she left and set off home, her limbs as heavy as lead and her eyes stinging with fatigue.

Lucy willed her lids to stay open as she negotiated the narrow lanes. Several times her wing mirror brushed bushes or clipped saplings, making her jump.

Once, she overshot a junction and stopped in the middle of it. Fortunately, nothing had been coming the other way.

She was too tired to drive safely and she realised that. But what could she do, stuck in the middle of the countryside?

Home was only a mile away now. She'd be OK as long as she slowed down and focused on the road.

But her comfortable bed kept pushing its way into her consciousness.

As soon as she got indoors she'd fall straight between the sheets, pull her duvet tight under her chin and . . .

Lucy jerked as a cyclist glanced off her wing and disappeared into a ditch.

With that physique and dark hair poking from under his helmet, it could only have been one person.

Rupert!

Lucy stamped on the brakes and gripped the steering-wheel hard.

'I've killed him!'

Once the vehicle had stopped she leaped out and rushed to where the back wheel of his bike was sticking up in the air.

Where was Rupert?

Near Disaster

Her chest heaving and her throat constricted, Lucy stepped up to the buckled wheel. The rest of the bicycle lay in a ditch.

She peered down through long grass and weeds, dreading what she would see.

'Rupert? Are you all right?' she called, praying as she waited for any response.

It seemed an age before his head appeared. He'd removed his helmet and dead leaves stuck out of his hair.

'I'm fine, no thanks to you!'

Her hand flew to her chest with relief.

'Is anything broken? Should I call an ambulance?'

'No,' he said irritably. 'Don't call an ambulance. Let me get out of this ditch.'

A foot appeared on the verge and with one swift movement he stood beside her, covered in mud.

He checked himself over, stretching and flexing each long limb in turn. He touched his toes and twisted left and right.

'Nothing broken.'

Lucy sagged with relief.

Rupert glared at her.

'What were you doing? Did you see me?'

'I'm so sorry. It was entirely my fault. I thought . . .' She couldn't bring herself to say the words.

His eyes, dark and cold, bored into her.

'You could have killed me!'

Suddenly his expression changed.

'Are you OK?'

She wasn't. Whereas earlier she'd been struggling to stay awake, standing upright was becoming a problem. She placed a hand on the bike wheel for support.

'I'm fine but yes, I could have killed you.'

'Fortunately, you didn't. My bike, on the other hand . . .' He glanced at it and his mouth set in a firm line.

'I'll pay for it,' Lucy blurted out. 'Get it fixed and send me the bill.'

He turned his attention back to her.

'Were you asleep at the wheel?'

Lucy knew she might have been.

'I . . . it's been a long day. Everything happened so quickly.' She took a deep breath. 'I'm so thankful you're not hur —'

Before she could finish the word the adrenaline spike from the collision wore off and the world blurred. Lucy put her hand to her head as everything tilted, darkened and the ground rushed up to meet her.

Suddenly his strong arm was around her waist, holding her upright.

'You're not fine. You're sick.'

He bent and picked her up. She put her arms around his neck to hold on.

'I'm sorry,' she muttered as he helped her into the passenger seat of her car.

'I'll drive. You're in no fit state.'

Lucy sank her head on to the headrest. Her eyes closed and her shoulders slumped.

The next thing she remembered was Rupert shaking her arm. They were at Longmeadow House.

'What are we doing here?' she asked, her tired eyes ranging over the cream masonry paint, dark green woodwork and long rows of mullioned windows.

He looked at her with concern.

'I asked if there was anyone at your home. Don't you remember?'

Lucy searched the fog of fatigue and shook her head.

'You're exhausted, perhaps more than that. I'll cook you supper and take you home afterwards. No arguments,' he added as she opened her mouth.

'This is all wrong,' she said as she climbed out of her car. 'I should be looking after you.'

Wake-Up Call

Sunlight streamed into the room. Puzzled, Lucy blinked a few times. Her bedroom had black-out curtains to help her fall back to sleep after early-morning, summer calls.

These curtains were of flimsy cotton and hung before mullioned windows.

Where was she? A small glass of clear liquid sat on a solid wood coffee table. She was on a faux leather sofa.

Lucy sat, pushing off a chenille throw, easing stiff neck and limbs and stretching as the events of last night fell into place.

Her heart thumped when she remembered the accident and saw Rupert ricocheting off her wing. Thank heavens he was OK.

He'd caught her when she nearly fainted and had driven her to his home. That was where she was — fully dressed, on his sofa.

'You're awake.'

Lucy looked towards the soft voice. Rupert leaned casually in the doorway.

He wore a light blue T-shirt which stretched across broad shoulders and pecs. Tanned, muscular legs stretched from loose shorts to the floor.

Lucy rose and folded the throw.

'This is embarrassing. I should go.'

'No, you should stay and eat the breakfast I'm cooking.'

Breakfast? She never had time for a cooked breakfast.

'What time is it?'

'Seven o'clock.'

At least she wasn't late. As she became aware of the smell of homemade bread and coffee her stomach growled.

When had she last eaten?

'It's too much, Rupert. I've already spent the night on your sofa.'

'You needed to. You crashed out before you even touched your G&T. I tried to wake you when supper was ready but you were dead to the world.

'I nearly called an ambulance for you.'

Lucy groaned. This was awful. She'd

nearly killed him and he'd brought her home and cooked for her. She'd rewarded him by sleeping right through!

'Come on, Lucy. You need a square meal and feeding people is what I do best.'

'What do you mean?' she asked.

'Didn't you know? I used to be a chef.'

'I believed you were a banker.'

'What made you think that?'

'Josie Grainger said you retired early from a job in the City.'

He stared at her for a few moments.

'That explains a lot. Well, it's partly true. I did run a restaurant in London. I'd two Michelin stars and a waiting list of three weeks just for lunches!'

He turned and cracked an egg into a pot of boiling water on a huge modern range.

'I haven't retired. I've left my old life behind.'

While Rupert cooked Lucy checked out the kitchen. It was huge with a traditional flag floor but it boasted fitted pine cupboards, a modern pine table and an aluminium, integrated draining-board and bowl.

'I'm making poached duck eggs with spinach and nutmeg on sourdough toast,' Rupert said. 'You're not allergic or anything, are you?'

Lucy's stomach growled again.

'No. Thank you. That sounds amazing.'

Much better than the toast and marmalade or breakfast bar she normally grabbed during her daily rush for the door.

She lifted one corner of a tea towel that covered a cooling rack, and her mouth fell open in astonishment.

'You've made fresh bread this morning?'

'I baked it, yes. Good sourdough takes a full day to mature. We won't be eating that this morning. It's far too fresh.'

Lucy leaned against the sink and stared out of the window at the gravel patio and neat rows of vegetables stretching off.

Rupert's lifestyle was everything hers was not — organised, wholesome and sustainable.

She gripped the edge of the sink and shut her eyes as she recalled the accident.

Caused by exhaustion, it was a literal wake-up call. She had been running on empty for too long. This had to change.

She shuddered to think what would have happened had a child come round the bend on his or her bike instead of Rupert.

She must sleep more and work less. She needed to look after herself better and still, somehow, keep her home and livelihood.

But how? She should talk to her father and Elaine when she found time.

No. That sort of thinking created this mess. She couldn't wait until she had time. She must make time.

'Penny for them?'

Lucy spun around.

'I owe you an explanation,' she began.

'I agree. I don't know what's driving you so hard, Lucy, but it can't go on.'

'I know. I've been trying to hold out . . . this last year's been . . .'

She sat at the table and breathed deeply.

'A couple of years ago the vet practice was thriving, with three partners. We expanded and took out a loan to enlarge the premises.

'My fiancé and I bought a house. Then Tony, the senior partner, got injured on a farm visit. Unexpected complications set in and he died.'

Lucy's voice wobbled as she related the awful news about the man who had been her idol since childhood. He could always find a smile no matter how grim the weather or the task ahead.

Rupert's expression softened.

'I'm sorry. Were you close?'

Lucy smiled grimly and nodded.

'I knew him all my life — he inspired me to become a vet. All I ever wanted to do was work at North Millton Veterinary Practice.'

'You work alone,' Rupert observed, dropping slices of bread into his toaster. 'What happened to the other partner?'

'Tony's son,' she stated matter-offactly. 'With his dad gone Jamie felt free to do what he'd always wanted to.

'Apparently he had only become a country vet to please his dad. He's in Florida now, working with alligators.'

Rupert's face registered shock.

'He left you with all that work?'

'And debt. Yes.'

'You're the only one in debt from this?'

'Yes and no. It's complicated. We'd split the loan three ways.

'Tony's insurance paid off that third. Jamie still owes his third, but, as he just inherited a bunch and sold his half of the house to me, that's not a problem for him.'

'Meanwhile you're working yourself into the ground to keep yourself afloat.'

'I'm searching for a new partner,' Lucy argued. 'I was only trying to hold out until August, when a newly qualified vet might join for a trial period.'

'Couldn't you get locums in?'

If only it was that simple.

'There's a vet shortage. Even if I can get someone to come work in the sticks they'll only do the small-animal stuff.

'I've never been frightened of hard work. My father was a farmer all his working life and when the going got tough he worked harder until things eased off again.

'It always came good for him. I assumed it would for me. But I realise now I can't carry on like this.'

'True,' Rupert said. 'I'll level with you, Lucy, I was thinking about informing the police.'

Lucy's heart rate spiked with dread, but she nodded.

'I wouldn't blame you.'

'I don't think it's the right decision for either of us. I'm already struggling to win hearts and minds around here.'

He paused and rolled his eyes.

'I can see why, if everyone thinks I'm a billionaire banker. They're all probably waiting for me to up sticks this autumn and spend the winter partying on my private yacht!

'Prosecuting the local vet won't help my image and it might be the last straw for you.'

Lucy's eyes filled up. It would absolutely be the last straw.

'I can't imagine how tough life has been,' Rupert continued. 'But I see a dedicated and talented vet.

'I don't want to take that away from you, Lucy, but I can't ignore what happened, either.'

'No,' she agreed. 'I need to change. And I will.'

'Just promise me you'll never let yourself get that tired again.'

As long as Lucy lived, she would never forget the moment she had sent this man flying through the air.

She looked up and met his gaze honestly and openly as a tear escaped down her cheek.

'I promise.'

Two Stolen Geese

'You should sell your food on your stall,' Lucy said between groans of delight over the delicious breakfast. 'You'd make a fortune. You could . . .'

She noticed the twinkle in Rupert's eye.

'Oh, you've thought of this already. Stupid of me.'

'Yes. Selling eggs and bits of veg won't pay the bills. I think you can help me.'

He took a tartlet from his American-style larder fridge.

'This was last night's tea. Take it home and tell me what you think.'

Lucy smiled. He was giving her doggy bags now? She took the tart anyway.

As she was leaving she received a text. Jack Turner wondered if she would see one of his geese on her way to work.

The presumption of the man! Jack's farm was not on her way to work. At least not from her house.

Did Jack know she'd spent the night at

Longmeadow? Had he been spying from his house, the roof of which was visible over a low rise on the other side of the valley?

She was about to reply that she'd certainly do that if he had a moment to pay his bills.

But it made sense to call on him now rather than return later. She set off, determined to tackle him about his debt.

Jack was a few years older than her dad. He was wiry with a thick, grey goatee and a lined face from a life lived outdoors.

Lucy struggled to keep up with him as he strode to the yard where he'd penned two large white geese.

One was limping.

'Are these new?' she asked.

He nodded.

'Thought they'd make a good burglar alarm after what happened to Uncle Fester. But look, the joint's swollen.'

Lucy had a bad feeling.

'Let's take a closer look.'

Jack soon had the bird firmly trapped

in his arms. Lucy reached for the large, orange foot and knew by a hole in the webbing plus the current medical complaint that she'd seen it before.

'I know what's wrong, Jack, but I'm sure these geese are stolen.'

'What? Pinched by the same people who took my horse?' He looked shocked.

She nodded.

'If I'm right, they're micro-chipped.'

'Who puts identity chips in poultry?'

She fetched her portable scanner which confirmed her suspicions.

'I'll take them to the clinic. It's possible the sanctuary they were taken from may let you keep them.' She hovered, willing herself to talk about money.

'I hope so, Lucy.' He took out a cotton handkerchief and wiped his eyes. 'I can't take any more knocks. Truly, I can't.'

Lucy's resolve crumbled. She didn't want to drive this man over the edge. She'd get Elaine to tackle him later.

★ ★ ★

Halfway through the morning surgery two police constables arrived for the geese. Lucy took them through to the holding area.

'Jack bought them in good faith,' she explained.

One of the PCs stood well back from their cage. Both looked nervous.

'They're enormous!'

'Yes. They're geese.'

They exchanged worried glances.

'Have we got facilities to keep them?'

'They can't stay here,' she said, straight-faced. 'They're evidence.

'They are well behaved and they'll be fine in the car with a seatbelt. Just make sure their heads are facing towards the buckle.'

Both men blanched. Lucy couldn't keep her face straight.

'I'm joking! They can stay here.'

After they'd gone Lucy texted Michael.

Another theft last night, came the reply to her text. *Silver 4x4 seen nearby. Near Knowle End. Your car wasn't outside your house. Was that you?*

Not me, she typed back, then wondered how he knew about her car. She lived at the far end of a cul-de-sac.

Why would Michael be passing her house late in the evening?

Three patients waiting. Lucy put her phone away and called in Desmond, a roly-poly cat with halitosis. She anticipated more dental work and owner education.

She put on a welcoming smile and wondered how to tackle his owner about Desmond's addiction to cheese and biscuits:

'He refuses to eat anything else, dear!"

The term 'pet psychologist' popped into Lucy's head. Elaine might have a point.

After another long day Lucy went home to Rupert's tartlet. She'd bought Frisée lettuce from Josie's and Jersey Royals. Only the best seemed right for Rupert's cooking.

The meal was divine, the pastry so thin it almost wasn't there, the filling a delicate blend of sorrel, thyme, lemon and more.

As she chased the last crumbs around her plate her thoughts strayed to the handsome incomer, the accident and the bike she needed to pay for somehow.

A text arrived.

How was the tart?

She failed to find suitable superlatives. *Let down by the salad*, she texted back.

Her phone rang.

'I'm glad you liked it.'

''Like' is not a strong enough word!'

'Good, because I want to ask a favour. As a busy working professional you represent my target market in many ways.

'Would you come over one evening to advise me which other dishes I should sell?'

A week ago she'd have refused for all sorts of reasons, including lack of time. But the new Lucy would make time, because it would be fun.

As Rupert's food was divine and she owed him a lot the reasons to accept vastly outnumbered those to decline.

They arranged a time. Lucy wondered

what small gift she could take with her to express gratitude for what he'd done. Giving an opinion on his food felt like a favour for her, not him.

She had an idea. But she'd need to talk to her dad about it.

Unusual Gift

Rupert threw open the front door and strode outside to welcome Lucy. She looked different — more relaxed and with colour in her cheeks.

Lemon Capri trousers and a flowery orange T-shirt showed off curves he hadn't realised she possessed. Without her Alice band her hair flowed around her face in a carefree holiday look.

He liked it a lot.

'I decided it was pointless bringing wine or chocolates for a chef so I brought these. You don't have to accept but Dad and I thought they'd be perfect for you.'

She opened her boot.

'You didn't need to —' he began but she shushed him with a hand.

Rupert saw eight fluffy bundles scrabbling about in a cardboard box. They had mottled brown plumages with off-white streaks.

'Wow! Are these Japanese quail?'

'Yep.'

'How did you know I wanted some?' In his delight he caught her by the arms and placed a grateful kiss on her cheek.

Lucy froze and he knew he'd overdone it. He stepped back.

'Sorry. I got carried away.'

'That's OK,' she said, turning to the box and lifting it out.

But there was no eye contact, so it wasn't OK. After what she'd told them the last time they met, Rupert remembered Lucy was emotionally fragile. He vowed to be more mindful of her vulnerability.

'I figured a chef could make great use of their little eggs,' she told him.

'I can! But you can't afford —'

'They didn't cost me a penny,' Lucy said. 'My dad breeds them and had more success than usual this spring.

'Anyway, this is a thank-you for helping his daughter the other day.'

At the front door Rupert pointed down.

'Leave them here for now. It's shaded. They'll be safe and it will remind me to take them to the stables when you leave.

'Thank your father. It's very thought-ful.'

Lucy put down the box and started to fold the flaps shut to keep the birds safe.

'Wait,' he said. 'I want to hold one.'

She turned inquisitive eyes to his and he gave a shrug. Lucy grinned.

'You're a big softy, aren't you?'

'Guilty as charged.'

He lifted one bird and held it to his chest. The tiny creature settled in his hands as though sensing there was no danger.

'How old are they?'

'Four weeks.'

'So they should start laying eggs in a few more weeks?'

Lucy nodded.

He needed to prepare a space for them fast. Somewhere secure but with room to roam and explore, plus a safe nesting area.

'When you've finished being gooey,' Lucy said, 'you did promise me food.'

Reluctantly he replaced the bird with its siblings, secured the top and led the way to the kitchen.

'Oh, my!' Lucy's eyes ranged across the feast he'd laid out on the table. 'You must have been baking for days!'

Rupert explained that he spent days or weeks planning but the actual cooking only took an afternoon. He told her he used seasonal local ingredients.

Now he was talking about what he did best he found it difficult to stop.

After washing his hands he produced a small plate, cutlery and a paper napkin and Lucy methodically helped herself.

'What's this?' she asked of the third tart.

'Nettle and crumbly Lancs cheese.' He studied her face. 'Is it the nettles? Are they a step too far?'

'It's fab! The flavours are sublime,' she replied. 'This one is a definite.'

A smile tugged at the corners of his mouth. He'd done well to ask Lucy.

The worst thing she could have done was love everything and be indecisive.

Instead she shared carefully-considered thoughts.

While they deliberated on final choices Rupert offered her homemade cordial.

After one sip she stared at the glass. 'What is this?'

'Elderflower.'

'Did you make it?'

Rupert nodded.

'Why? Don't you like it?'

'I love it!' Lucy took another sip. 'You must turn up with this. Seriously! If the weather's hot people will drink gallons.'

He hadn't planned to offer drinks but, with elderflowers free and plentiful, it would provide a decent return.

His remaining cash had been carefully budgeted for. Longmeadow had to turn a profit as he'd no other source of income.

'I'll add it to my list,' he told her.

'What will you do with the leftovers?' she asked, hungry eyes zig-zagging over the remaining food.

'Freeze them for my volunteers.'

Rupert watched her face fall. It thrilled

him to see how much she loved his cooking. He held up a paper bag and grinned.

'But I can spare a doggy bag.'

Those remarkable grey eyes sparkled as she took the bag. His heartbeat accelerated, and he tore his attention away, washing her plate instead of watching her help herself.

Making this woman smile shouldn't make him this happy and he mustn't let that feeling get out of control. He didn't want a repeat of what had happened between him and Amelia. It was why he had left his previous life behind.

He must focus his energy on setting up his permaculture system and partnering local sustainability networks.

'What volunteers?' Lucy's question broke into his thoughts.

'Didn't I say? Six people are coming in two weekends to help me with bigger projects I'd struggle to do on my own.'

'For free?'

He nodded.

'It's part of the permaculture sharing-and-caring ethos. That's why I needed a place the size of Longmeadow House. I'll have to put them up.

'They'll learn about permaculture . . .' he gestured to the table '. . . and eat gourmet food.'

Lucy clutched her doggy bag tight.

'Can anyone turn up and get fed as long as they muck in?'

'I would love you to join us, whether you muck in or not.'

He'd consider it part of his project to help Lucy. The change in her after a few days was remarkable.

Her beauty was blooming, which suggested she was keeping her side of their bargain and had changed her ways.

By spending time at Longmeadow, hopefully she'd continue to relax and heal.

Asking Lucy to spend time here would be purely in her own interest. He had to remember that.

Her gaze strayed through the window.

'I've always lived in North Millton and I've coveted this place since I was a vet student, but until you called me to see Alison I'd never set foot in Long-meadow.'

Rupert knew a cue when he heard one. 'Would you like a tour?'

She spun around with shining eyes.

'Would you mind? Ja — my ex and I didn't view it when we were house-hunting. We decided not to torture ourselves.'

Interesting. Had Lucy been about to say Jamie? Had she been engaged to the partner who left for America?

Losing two partners and the love of your life must have left a huge hole in her life. No wonder she was hurting so much and filling that hole with overwork.

He held open the kitchen door.

'Let's get the ducks inside.'

Lucy gasped as they headed out. Rupert knew that sound well — he made it every morning when he threw back the curtains and took in the view.

Some called Yorkshire God's own county but he decided they were people who hadn't seen Lancashire.

With pride he talked about what he'd achieved so far with his veg and herb beds. He walked her through the large polytunnel, bursting with heat-loving plants such as squash and tomatoes.

'You've achieved so much in two months,' Lucy marvelled.

'I moved in with a carload of seedlings and an overnight case.'

'What next?' she asked, looking at a wilder area he hadn't tackled yet.

'My volunteers will help me tame this lot.' He described the path he wished to lay, the saplings that needed removing and much more.

'It's the first of many such weekends, I hope,' he finished.

They'd reached the gate to the duck field. Lucy peered over.

Gabriel, the drake, danced expectantly on tip-toe, his ladies following suit about him.

She laughed and unlatched the gate.

'These guys are hungry!'

The ducks rushed through and crowded Rupert who was holding a jug of wheat.

'I've missed this,' she told him as they

headed for the stables, ducks darting between their legs, parping furiously. 'It was my job to feed the chickens on our farm when I was a little girl. I loved it.'

Once the ducks were safely in their stall they toured the house. Then he escorted her to her car, encouraging her again to visit during his volunteer weekend.

'I'll be on call,' she answered, 'so I'll probably be too busy. I won't have time to get my hands dirty.'

'Not even for goats'-cheese-and-walnut salad with salt-encrusted, baked new potatoes?'

He saw temptation written over her lovely face and fought back the urge to kiss her again, not on her cheek but her lips.

Rupert watched her silver Subaru retreat down the lane and he turned back to the house. He needed to prepare a temporary home for the quail.

He'd have another cuddle first, though. Smiling, he reached down. And found nothing.

The quail had gone.

Searching for Clues

'I don't understand it,' Rupert said again. 'Where did they go?'

Lucy shook her head. His frantic text had made her turn the car round and drive right back to Longmeadow.

'We did put them here, didn't we?'

Rupert nodded.

'Let's look around. Maybe someone's playing a trick. Or one of us had a mad moment and moved them without registering it.'

'You believe that?' he asked.

Lucy shook her head.

'No, but I'm struggling to believe that someone walked on to your property and stole them without us noticing.'

'We spent ages at the other end of the house and in the garden,' he reminded her, looking towards the polytunnel. 'Anyone could have sneaked in.'

But who would do that, she wondered. And why?

They searched methodically in the

gathering gloom — every room, every outhouse, all corners of the garden and his fields. Nothing.

Lucy phoned Michael, who listened but sounded sceptical.

'It sounds like a different perpetrator to me, Lucy. The other thefts happened at night.

'Are you sure this guy's not attention-seeking? You don't even know him.'

It was true, she didn't know Rupert like she knew Michael, but only a magician could have hidden the box so quickly and effectively!

'We checked everywhere, Michael. The quail aren't here.'

He gave a weary sigh.

'I'll notify the team and try to call in the next few days.'

Lucy disconnected the call and turned to Rupert, frustrated.

'Why isn't he taking this more seriously? The thief was here within the last hour or two.

'You'd think he'd be straight over, looking for clues!' she added.

'It's hardly a murder, is it?' Rupert answered. 'Though, to be honest, I feel so bad that it might as well have been.'

Lucy felt awful, too. She'd give anything to turn the clock back and put the box somewhere safer.

'It's down to us. Come on.'

She headed for the lane which ran past Longmeadow. The parking area lay directly off it and the front door was a mere 20 feet from the tarmac.

'Where are we going?'

'To search for clues. Transpose Longmeadow to Midsomer and pretend you're Inspector Barnaby.'

'I hope it doesn't mean I'll find a corpse!'

Rupert attempted a grin which failed to hide the worry in his eyes. Lucy had seen that look before, on the first day she'd attended to Alison.

He'd been outwardly confident but she saw the caring, worried man beneath.

She wanted to reassure him now, as she had that first day, but to do more than lay a hand on his arm.

She turned her attention back to the road and ordered herself to focus. Apart from the roof of Jack Turner's farm there was no house in sight.

No walkers, nothing.

However, Longmeadow lay low in the valley with lots of blind spots.

Rupert stood next to her at the edge of the road. As they gazed out at the surrounding countryside Lucy strove to block out her awareness of the man standing next to her — his warmth, his caring, his vulnerability.

The ground was parched after an unusually dry spring. Even using the torch from her phone she saw nothing useful.

'It's hopeless, Lucy. They're gone.'

The disappointment on his face tugged at something deep inside her. His little-boy-lost expression was irresistible.

Before she could stop herself she stepped forward and threw her arms around him. He hesitated for a second, then his arms circled her, too.

The embrace was all she'd imagined it would be, his body yielding yet strong.

She took a breath and his scent, sandal-wood with a hint of masculinity, filled her.

This was what she'd missed every night since Jamie left. Wrapped in Rupert's arms she felt nothing could harm her because he wouldn't let it.

She wanted this feeling to last for ever. She wanted to close her eyes and forget her troubles. When she opened them again, everything would be fine — the storm would be over and the sun would be shining.

'Tell your father I'm sorry,' he whispered, his breath brushing her ear like the softest of kisses.

She eased away from him, her gaze searching his face.

'Why?'

His eyes remained troubled.

'I lost his chicks. I knew there was a thief about and I left them in plain sight.

'I should have taken them inside or straight to the stables. I just hope who-ever took those defenceless little birds doesn't hurt them.'

His words and his expression sparked anger in Lucy.

'It wasn't just you, Rupert. I put them there — I left them. Don't blame yourself for what some troublemaker has done.'

'But —'

'Look,' she added sternly, 'you should be able to leave a cardboard box by your own front door for an hour! I've never known anything like this happen here before.'

She turned towards her car and beeped off the alarm.

'If Michael isn't going to do anything then I will.'

'Where are you going?'

'To question your neighbours.'

She hurried away before their mutual sense of loss and confusion led to more intimacy she would later regret.

She parcelled up those negative feelings into the mental box where she tried to corral all her other woes and then channelled her emotions into action.

Someone needed to conduct door-to-door enquiries yet the police seemed uninterested.

After checking at every house along the lane within half a mile of Longmeadow she returned home frustrated.

Nobody had seen anything unusual. Those birds had disappeared into thin air.

She texted this lack of news to Rupert and switched on the kettle, wondering how else she might investigate these thefts now they had become very personal.

Her thoughts turned to Jack Turner. She hadn't called on him because his house stood well back at the end of a long track.

It was unlikely he'd have seen any unusual activity on the road. But even if he hadn't witnessed anything this evening he had personal information about the geese and Uncle Fester's disappearance that the police, including Michael, wouldn't share with her.

She formed a plan. The animal refuge had agreed to let Jack keep the geese.

Tomorrow she'd return them and have 'a chat' while she was there.

Satisfied there were more avenues for her to explore Lucy switched off the kettle, made some hot milk instead and headed upstairs to bed.

That Cheating Chap

'You found them on a pet website, then?' Lucy asked Jack early the following morning. 'What happened next?'

'The owner said he lived in the South Lakes. He dropped them off with my sister in Lancaster and she brought them over a few days later.'

'Is that how you normally buy livestock?'

'No, but these birds were going cheap for a quick sale. I needed cheering up after Uncle Fester went missing so I thought, why not get a couple of birds as pets?

'And maybe I wanted a burglar alarm after what happened.'

That made sense. It was certainly cheaper than installing an electronic system.

'Did your sister see the man who dropped them off?'

'It were dark. She said he were medium height with no accent. That's it, really.'

Not Rupert, then, whatever Michael thought.

'Age?'

'Thirty to forty. Why don't you ask her?'

He pulled out his phone and soon Lucy was talking to a woman called Loretta who spoke in a very posh, over-refined voice.

She confirmed Jack's story, adding little other than the man drove an estate car that might have been black.

Lucy thanked Loretta and turned to Jack.

'I presume you tried to contact the vendor after you learned they were stolen?'

He nodded.

'He's vanished from the website. Not surprising. My wife says it's easy enough to make a fake account and then disappear.'

Jack's wife taught IT at the local technical college.

'I presume you've looked for Uncle Fester on similar websites?' Lucy asked finally.

Jack looked thoughtful.

'It didn't cross my mind but you might have a point.' He grinned. 'We could catch the thief in one of them sting operations, couldn't we? Turner and Pugh, detectives extraordinaire. That would serve 'em right.'

Lucy smiled. She was about to leave when she remembered to ask about the quail.

'Someone took them from outside the door around eight or nine,' she finished.

Jack looked surprised.

'In daylight? Cheeky beggars!'

'Exactly. Did you spot any activity near the house?'

'Actually, I did go to the field where I kept Uncle Fester about that time. I were feeling right sorry for meself and moped at the gate awhile. I suppose I was hoping I'd made a mistake and he'd come galloping over from some hidden corner.

'I do remember a silver car parked outside Longmeadow House.'

'That was mine,' Lucy explained. 'I dropped the birds off.'

'I wondered.'

Lucy had the impression he'd known it was her car. She did not intend to explain how someone stole the birds while she was 'just dropping them off'.

Gossip multiplied like rabbits in these parts. If she admitted she'd been there half the evening Josie would have them halfway down the aisle in no time.

Jack continued.

'Two other cars were parked down by the river. Walkers often stop there.'

'Did you notice any people?'

'Yes. A young couple on this side of the valley and a hiker on the footpath which skirts that Cheating chap's half-acre field. A skinny person in shorts.

'Looked like they'd stopped to take some photos. It's a bonnie spot there. You can see halfway to Bickerston.'

Lucy gritted her teeth at the description of Rupert as 'that Cheating chap'.

'A man or a woman?'

Jack shrugged.

'Couldn't tell. They were too far away.'

As Lucy drove away she was tempted

to stop at Longmeadow to see how Rupert was holding up after the previous evening's drama. She decided not to.

Who knew how long it would take her to escape Rupert's welcoming kitchen again? And if they hugged again to console each other, where might that lead?

Lucy was on the edge of a slippery slope. It would be easy to fall in love with him but she had no intention of risking her heart again so soon — certainly not until she'd resolved her other problems.

Michael's warning last night picked away at the edge of her consciousness, too.

This theft was different. How well did she really know Rupert?

And why would a highly successful chef suddenly give that life up to live off the land hundreds of miles away from friends and family?

Rupert was, in many respects, still a dark horse.

So she skipped Longmeadow and drove straight to work.

Is He the Thief?

Michael, in uniform, was waiting for her when she arrived.

'Aren't you working at Forrest's today?' she asked, referring to the outdoor clothing and equipment shop named after its owner — Niall Forrest.

'Niall's let me go,' Michael said, too casually. 'He's struggling with on-line competition.'

Lucy switched her computer on then shot her friend a sympathetic look.

'I'm sorry, Michael. When did that happen?'

'Few weeks ago.'

Lucy looked at him sharply.

'And you didn't tell me?'

He shrugged but didn't make eye contact with her.

'It's no big deal. I'll find something else.'

Now Lucy thought about it she should have realised he would normally have been at the shop, that time he called at

Rupert's house about Uncle Fester's disappearance.

'What will you do?'

Michael rubbed his finger distractedly back and forth along the edge of the examination table.

'I'll be fine. I've got contacts and skills. I've applied to the regular police.

'But I haven't come to talk about me.'

He stopped fidgeting and looked at Lucy.

'I came about your father's quail. I rang Rupert Chetwynd. He tells me you were there for several hours.'

Although he presented this as a simple checking of facts Lucy sensed he was questioning how she spent her spare time and with whom.

She turned back to the computer.

'Yes,' she said briefly.

It was none of his business what she and Rupert had been doing.

For a few moments he didn't answer.

'You two seem to be getting close.'

Lucy focused on the screen.

'He's a nice chap with great ideas

about the environment. I like him and we both need friends right now. But he is just a friend, Michael.'

He moved half a step closer. Lucy stared at the screen but his presence unsettled her, like thunderclouds looming over the horizon.

'I'm worried about you, Lucy. You haven't got over Jamie and I won't see you hurt again. We know nothing about this guy.

'He could be the thief.'

Lucy faced him, not understanding why he had this fixation.

'Do you honestly believe he stole his own property?'

Michael shrugged.

'It wouldn't be the first time. He could be using the other thefts as cover.'

'That's ridiculous!'

'Don't get too close, Lucy. That's all I'm saying.'

Michael's hand rested on her shoulder now. She supposed he meant it to be reassuring.

Gently she removed his hand.

'How did you know I wasn't at home the night the geese disappeared?'

Michael backed off slightly, his brows puckered in confusion.

'I — I was training. I'm doing an ultra-marathon next month, remember?

'Your road is on my run route. I carry on along the bridle path then down to the canal.'

His explanation made sense. Michael ran and cycled as often as other people went to the pub. A long, straight cinder path, popular with runners, led from the end of her modern cul-de-sac to the next village.

She relaxed. She'd been over-thinking things. How likely was it that her special constable friend, whom she'd known since school, would stalk her?

Jamie had left her head in more of a mess than she liked to admit.

She turned back to the computer to finish setting up for surgery.

'Don't worry about me, Michael. I won't trust any man for a long time.'

Suddenly he grasped her elbow. She

turned her head and their gazes locked.

The air between them stilled and, her heart racing, she knew he was about to say something personal. Something she preferred not to hear.

Since Jamie left something had changed between them but Lucy had ignored it, not wanting to confront the truth.

Michael wanted more than she was prepared to give. He was a friend she didn't want to lose but, even if she was ready to trust again, she knew she'd never feel the same way in his arms as she had in Rupert's.

Time slowed and the air grew thick with tension.

As Michael opened his mouth to speak there was a knock on the door and Elaine marched in.

Tougher Approach

The Saturday morning emergency surgery dragged. A few appointments for small pets and no-visit requests meant Lucy's stress levels rose though her bank account didn't.

Over the last week or so she'd achieved a lot. She'd stopped doing late visits, passing them to whoever was on call for the rota she shared with the Bickerston vets instead.

She'd also reduced her nights on call and had arranged a little financial wiggle room by talking to Jamie's mum about rent on their two-thirds of the premises.

She'd been given an update on her ex.

'Best you hear it from me, Lucy, not someone like Josie Grainger.'

Lucy was grateful to be told but, in all honesty, didn't know how to feel about it.

She had more sleep and more energy but she needed work to be busy during the day if she were to avoid financial disaster.

Between appointments she searched the internet for stolen animals, starting with the quail her father had gifted to Rupert.

She found some Japanese quail, the sort her father bred, but not eight of them.

Next she sought a Tamworth boar. Logically that beast would be sausages by now: old-breed products fetched high prices and were harder to trace than a living animal.

They might pop up on an artisanal meat stall near Rupert's. Another reason to visit the farmer's market.

She couldn't find a bay stallion with a white blaze, either.

After working through the list of missing animals, interrupted by a cat with a cough and a pregnant gerbil, she gave up.

It was nearly lunchtime. Nina, the receptionist, came through to discuss a visit request.

'It's Mrs Brookes again,' she said with an eye roll.

Lucy stared at her.

'Not her Pekingese?'

Nina nodded.

'I saw them in Josie's shop yesterday. The dog seemed fine,' Lucy mused.

'Shall I tell her she has to come in?'

Sadie Brookes habitually justified a home visit for Paddington the Peke on what seemed perfectly reasonable grounds. But when Lucy arrived he was never as ill as described.

Sadie was on her list of debtors, too, always pleading poverty despite living in an immaculately kept, semi-detached house.

'Has she paid her last bill yet?'

Nina shook her head.

'What's wrong with Paddington this time?'

'Colic.' Nina gave another eye roll. 'He's probably pinched a pickled onion.'

A month ago Lucy would have accepted the visit without question. She believed it was her role to provide an excellent service to the community she lived in and loved.

Now, however, she accepted she had to work smarter to protect herself and safeguard the practice.

Besides, from past experience Nina's diagnosis might be right.

'Tell her I'm far too busy to visit today. She has to bring Paddington in and pay her outstanding bill on arrival,' she told Nina. 'Remind her it's much cheaper to come in than have a home visit.'

'Yes!' Nina punched the air and turned back to Reception.

It seemed Elaine wasn't alone in thinking Lucy should be tougher with the clients.

They were right; Lucy saw that now. In her grief and determination she had been thinking entirely along rigid lines.

Or perhaps she hadn't been thinking at all, just ploughing blindly on.

This was the new, more assertive Lucy, who would occasionally challenge demanding clients.

Besides, the way Sadie Brookes acted whenever Lucy visited made her feel like a servant.

'Come to the back door. Take your shoes off.'

'Don't sit there, that's Paddington's chair.'

When Mrs Brookes and Paddington arrived Lucy walked through to the Reception to collect them.

'This place is going downhill.' Sadie shot a vitriolic look at Nina from beneath a perfectly coiffed and dyed bob.

'Tony would never have demanded money from me before seeing Paddington!'

Lucy ruffled Paddington's ear. The Peke wagged his tail, his tongue protruding as usual from what appeared a smiling mouth.

'If they haven't settled the previous bill then, yes, we ask people to pay first.

'You're free to use the vets in Bickerston,' she added.

When Mrs Brookes didn't reply Lucy led her through to her clinical room.

'Right. What are we doing for this gorgeous boy?'

Farmer's Market

Finally her workload was clear, the patients all seen and the notes finished. The Bickerston vets were on call for the rest of the weekend, leaving Lucy's afternoon free.

She could go anywhere and do anything she liked. But where?

A ton of cleaning awaited her at home and the lawn was several weeks past a good cut. She usually visited her father over the weekend when time allowed, too.

But the farmer's market beckoned, with stalls harbouring illicit Tamworth pork sausages, perhaps. She would also see Rupert with his mouth-watering produce.

She drove into town and parked near the river, then headed uphill to the old sheep market in the central square. It was surrounded by almost-unchanged Georgian and Victorian stone buildings.

The Saturday market straggled up the

hill and around the edges of the square. Lucy passed artisan bakers, cheese-mongers, farmers, honey sellers and handicraft stalls all doing a brisk trade beneath awnings of all shapes, sizes and colours.

Eventually she spotted Rupert behind a wall of customers. She gaped at the scrum.

Rupert looked up and saw her. From the panic in his eye and hair more ruffled than usual Lucy concluded he was not coping.

So, she thought, he was human!

He beckoned her over.

'Just a moment,' he said to his customers. 'My assistant has arrived.'

Assistant? Bemused, Lucy slid behind the stall and dropped her handbag into some empty boxes.

'I want a half-dozen duck eggs and two of those rhubarb things.' The woman had a posh voice and an African-print scarf tied around her head.

'Of course.'

Lucy scanned the stall for the relevant

items. Rupert pointed to them without breaking off from his own customer.

'Do you, um, have a bag?' she asked the lady.

'No.'

Now what? Lucy looked around wildly.

'Paper bags for the tubs of rhubarb crumble,' Rupert told her, 'and I've some used carrier bags under the table.'

Lucy slid the crumbles into the little bags and put everything into a slightly creased supermarket bag. She took the money but before she had time to pat herself on the back an elderly gent wearing a tweed suit demanded three sorrel tarts.

So it continued all afternoon.

'I'm exhausted!' she said when the market finally closed and they took a moment to relax.

She rested on a small folding stool Rupert had brought with him. He leaned against a bollard a few feet away.

'I have never been so pleased to see someone! I'm ecstatic that my produce was so popular but I was drowning when you arrived. Ten more minutes and the mob might have breached the barricades!'

Lucy chuckled.

'I'm not surprised, with the prices you charged. Sixty pence for one of your exquisite tartlets! Seriously?'

'I wanted to keep prices low until word gets around and demand builds up. I expected to have lots unsold as I haven't built up a reputation yet.'

'I presume you told Josie Grainger your plans,' Lucy guessed. 'She's the best free advertising a man can buy.'

'Guilty as charged.'

Rupert grinned, making Lucy's stomach flip. He was the most attractive man she'd ever met and the look had seemed curiously intimate.

'Didn't you see any of the free samples I left with her for customers to try?' he added.

Lucy shook her head.

'I've taken packed lunches to work.'

It didn't take a mathematician to work out that two pounds a day for sandwiches added up to ten pounds a week.

His expression became serious.

'I really am pleased you're here. I thought you wouldn't come and I've no-one else I can count on yet. I'm still at the very early stage of building networks.'

'Networks sounds very businesslike. Are you sure you weren't a banker?'

'Mostly social networks,' he explained. 'Friends and neighbours I can rely on for help and support. You said yourself that I can't do it on my own.'

Was he hinting Lucy needed support, too?

'I also aim to start a co-operative where like-minded producers can pool resources and products. Set up bartering systems and perhaps even some sales venues, too.'

'You should talk to my father. He knows people and he'll chat about keeping poultry all day long.'

Rupert looked surprised and pleased.

'I'd love to meet him — as long as he doesn't mind.'

'Why should he mind?'

'I lost his —'

Lucy held up a hand.

'Those birds were stolen, Rupert. You did not lose them.'

'I know but that's not how it feels. I should have put them safely inside.'

'I could have put them safely inside, too.'

She pulled out her phone.

'Shall I'll send him your number?'

'Yes, please.' Rupert sighed. 'This afternoon keeps getting better. Are you free every other Saturday?'

Lucy laughed. He was pushing his luck although there were definitely worse ways of spending her free time. She felt happier than she had in months.

'How about if I repay your help with food?' he asked.

Lucy looked over the few items that remained on the stall. They were mostly vegetables that she'd no idea how to cook.

'Tempting, but no.'

'I mean supper at my place.'

'Oh. Tonight?'

'Yes. You'll be doing me another favour. I miss having friends and family around me.'

Lucy could think of many reasons to accept and only one reason to decline. But that one was huge.

She stared at Rupert, looking so very handsome, as she waited for this mental see-saw to settle one way or the other.

Sowing the Seeds

Rupert prepared a fresh herb vinaigrette to dress the salad he'd asked Lucy to pick from his kitchen garden.

When he invited her to visit him at the stall he'd anticipated a friendly chat, maybe fetching him a coffee, not pitching in and staying all afternoon. But it was a godsend she had. He'd been swamped.

The success of his stall was down to her, too. If she hadn't told him what local people had assumed about his past he'd have carried on hiding his credentials and expecting his cooking to speak for itself.

He wasn't sure why he had been so cagey about his past, other than wishing to avoid opening a can of worms. But if people had asked why he'd sold his restaurant and headed north surely he could have answered without sharing all the painful details.

It was those details that held him back

from even attempting to start a relation-ship with Lucy.

He watched her approach the back door with a basket of mixed salad leaves. Her cheeks were rosy and her light brown hair with blonde and red tints glittered in the early evening sun.

Her body curved naturally and her hips swayed easily. Everything about her spoke of happiness and contentment.

The tension and sheer determination to keep putting one foot in front of the other had vanished. Rupert wanted to see her like this all the time.

As she approached he automatically reached out to remove a smudge of dirt from her nose. Her eyes widened in surprise and possibly something else.

He made himself continue the action — drawing back would make things more awkward. He showed her the smudge on his fingertip.

'Honestly!' he said, making light of the intimate touch. 'It's like having a child about the place.'

After a few tense seconds she grinned.

'I got a spider on my nose. Brrr! Had to brush it off.'

Just like that the tension vanished.

He examined the leaves in her basket.

'Great choices. Run cold water in a bowl and dunk them to ensure they don't wilt and to wash off any bugs and soil.'

'Aye, aye, sir.' She gave a mock salute.

After she'd rinsed the leaves Rupert shooed her away from his cooking area while he made the omelette and assembled and dressed the salad.

With a small glass of dry white wine as an apéritif he dispatched her to set the table.

'You won't just sit and relax, will you?'

She shook her head.

'It's the farmer's daughter in me — if anyone's working it should be me.'

Ten minutes later they sat at one corner of the great kitchen table. Rupert was rewarded with blissful looks and groans as Lucy tucked into his food.

'This omelette is so light!' she said between mouthfuls. 'Broad beans and goat's cheese? I'd never have thought of it.

'I don't like broad beans. Or I thought I didn't. What did you do to them?'

To Rupert this was a simple meal prepared simply.

'Most people dislike the tough outer cover of the beans. If you boil them for a few minutes and extract the inner bean, you transform the taste.'

'I thought everyone knew that,' he added with a cheeky grin.

'You're talking to someone whose culinary prowess amounts to reading the instructions on the side of the packet.'

Lucy held up a speckled green and red leaf on her fork.

'As for lettuce, I don't know where to start. This isn't iceberg, is it?'

He rattled off a list of the different leaves, illustrating each with the relevant leaf.

'The choice was yours, though.'

'I picked what looked pretty!'

Rupert laughed.

'Honestly,' Lucy continued, 'if it hasn't a label I haven't got a clue. I've never grown salad.' She looked wistful.

'Buy a packet of seeds and throw them in the soil. See what comes up.'

'Tempting, but when do I have time? If you gave me self-sowing seeds that weeded and picked themselves I'd be in heaven.'

The statement struck Rupert profoundly. Lucy had no time to sow seeds yet she had found four hours to help him today and was still here now.

He wanted to thank her more personally, to say how he appreciated her effort and enjoyed her company, but couldn't think of the right form of words.

'How do you unwind when you get the chance?' he asked instead.

She blew out a big breath.

'I get hardly any chance. When I do there's cleaning and washing and shopping. You know, life stuff.'

'You don't have a cleaner?'

'If things were different I'd love a cleaner!'

Why couldn't she hire someone for a few hours a week? Then he remembered their previous conversation.

'Is money really so tight?'

Her cheeks grew pink.

'I'm considering taking in a lodger, something I would never have done a few weeks ago. My home is my castle and all that,' she finished with a shrug.

'I'm sorry, I had no idea. So working fewer hours isn't an option?'

Again, she shook her head.

'I've reduced visits I can get out of, I'm working smarter and I've talked to the bank since our encounter on the lane.

'It's helping but I love my job. I wouldn't want to do anything else.'

'I used to love my job, too,' he muttered.

She looked directly into his gaze.

'What changed?'

He realised too late he was straying into that area he'd been avoiding since he got here.

'It's a long story. The very short version is my marriage suffered a significant, um, issue. It led to my wife and me realising we both wanted different things.

'The decision to part was tough but

undoubtedly we did the right thing.'

What an understatement that was. Amelia still desperately wanted children while he could no longer take the stress of it all.

It only seemed a few short years ago Rupert had ached to have a family, too. Discovering that would never happen had been devastating.

He'd reconciled himself to it now but it didn't lessen his pain.

'It made me reassess what I want out of life. I realised I want to live at a slower pace,' he continued, glossing over a couple of devastatingly stressful years. 'One less environmentally damaging which helps safeguard the world for future generations.'

'She wanted something else?'

Lucy cocked her head to one side. A few strands of hair fell across her face and he had to restrain himself from moving them away with his finger.

He concentrated on his food.

'Yes and no. It's incredibly complicated.'

He admired Amelia's strength for continuing to follow her dream and he was pleased she'd achieved that with her new partner.

He hoped the choices he made helped ensure the world was a better place for them all.

To Lose a Soul Mate

'It's a tremendous leap, from top chef to living off the land,' Lucy commented.

'Not really,' Rupert replied. 'I always used in-season, fresh produce. I sourced locally to minimise air miles and carbon emissions.

'That meant my menu changed weekly, sometimes daily. No leek soup in the middle of summer or aubergine parmigiana in the depths of winter! And I loved to forage.'

Lucy laughed.

'You were practically there already, then, it seems.'

He smiled and shook his head.

'Only in my head. Though I did shut the restaurant down for a month in the quiet summer period and we took long-haul flights to all the top eco-tourism destinations — African safaris; the Inca trail; the orangutan sanctuary in Bor-neo.'

Lucy adopted a wistful look.

'They sound wonderful. We holidayed in Mexico one summer before Jamie and I took on the partnership. Oh, I . . . !'

Rupert guessed she hadn't planned to reveal quite so much about the disaster that had befallen her. That her absent work partner had also been her partner in life.

'It's OK,' he said. 'I worked out that you and Jamie were together. Had you been with him a long time?'

Lucy held out her wine glass for a refill; for courage, he assumed. He topped her up.

'We got together in the second year of university. Sixteen years ago.'

Her voice died away and she lowered her eyes and began to fiddle with the stem of her glass.

'Until he left to work with alligators?' Rupert prompted.

Lucy nodded.

'But you had known him for longer than that.'

He realised he was trying to tamp down the anger that flared inside him, anger directed at the man who had selfishly dumped this girl and had caused her so much grief.

Lucy nodded wearily.

'Since infant school.'

'Yet you had no idea he wanted to be an exotic vet?'

A shake of the head this time, followed by a sniff.

Rupert gave her hand a reassuring squeeze. She didn't pull away.

'You don't have to talk about it.'

'No, it's OK, it's not a secret. You would hear about it eventually in this place. Better it comes from me.'

She lifted her head to look at him, her eyes moist.

'And he's not exotic; he treats exotic animals. There's a big difference,' she finished with a defiant grin.

Rupert's mood lifted a little. If she could joke she was all right.

'You lived together?' he asked softly, still holding her hand.

He should break the connection — he'd held it for far too long. But it was acceptable for friends to hold hands, wasn't it?

Besides, Lucy was making no effort to remove her hand.

'We had everything,' she replied simply. 'A house, a life, a job we both loved. Or so I thought.'

She gave another ironic laugh.

'It was only a matter of time before we got married and started a family. It turned out that he was only staying in North Millton to please his dad.

'After Tony passed away the truth came out. Jamie loved exotic animals more than he loved me.'

Rupert released her hand. Of course Lucy wanted a family.

He balled both into fists on the table.

'I'd like to catch hold of this guy and shake him so hard!'

It was true.

The man had led Lucy on and caused her terrible pain. Focusing on this anger helped Rupert forget his own disappointment.

There was a pause, then a laugh.

'Me, too.'

This time it was Lucy who covered his hand with hers.

'Thank you for listening.'

He moved away as soon as she released him and collected the empty plates to make way for dessert.

'I understand what it's like to find your soul mate only to lose them again,' he told her from the safety of the other side of the room. 'Any time you need to unload I'm here.'

* * *

'Any time you need to unload.'

How many times did those words from Rupert echo through Lucy's head in the following week?

She couldn't 'unload' to Michael, at least not too often or too deeply, because she needed to maintain an emotional distance from him.

She had to remain strong in front of Elaine and the other staff.

Her father would make a few sympathetic noises and then show her round the quail pens as though that solved everything.

As for her sister, an eight-hour time difference meant having to plan chats well in advance.

The week passed in another blur of work.

As she rose the following Saturday morning, with an entire weekend on call ahead of her and a lawn that still needed cutting, her thoughts returned to Longmeadow and the volunteers.

They would be there now, helping and learning. If she popped round, as Rupert had invited her, she'd learn how permaculture worked and also feast on goat's cheese-and-walnut salad.

What did she have in the fridge? A pot of supermarket chicken soup.

What would he say to that? She imagined his warm smile and pictured those broad shoulders, so good for crying on.

Might she go to Longmeadow House if her work was quiet? He and Lucy

would be surrounded by volunteers.
What could possibly happen?

New Friends

Saturday began with a letter from the bank about a missed loan payment.

Over breakfast an urgent call about an injured sheep had Lucy leaping into her car, then arriving late and flustered for the emergency surgery.

Barely two hours later she failed to save Buster, a young dog involved in a car collision. His owner had rushed him to surgery with hope in her eyes and faith in her heart but ended up consoling Lucy.

'I know you did your best,' the woman said as they hugged each other. 'You can't save every animal and he went quickly. He didn't suffer long.'

True, but why did he have to leave this world so early? Lucy tried not to think about the ebullient puppy she remembered, all wagging tail and fevered licks.

As the last patient left Nina, the receptionist, entered Lucy's room.

'Are you all right?'

Lucy looked at her through wet eyes. Nina crossed the room and threw her arms around her in a big hug.

'You should go home and do something you enjoy,' Nina advised.

Lucy blew her nose and stared bleakly at the computer. What did she enjoy doing at home these days? Nothing.

'I have been invited out this afternoon,' she admitted. 'To Rupert Chetwynd's for lunch and to meet his volunteers. I'll go there.'

The fact was, even though she felt it prudent to avoid Longmeadow where possible, she felt better after a visit there. And today she definitely needed that.

Nina rubbed her shoulder.

'Great idea. You can tell us all about it on Monday. Is there anything else or shall we shut up shop?'

★ ★ ★

The volunteers were eating lunch at Rupert's picnic table on the limestone chipping area outside the kitchen door.

As Lucy rounded the side of the house cheerful chatter greeted her.

Rupert had his back to her, his wavy hair and broad shoulders instantly recognisable. He was sharing a joke with a young man sitting next to him.

Flutters in her stomach reminded Lucy she was a stranger today.

A woman with short pink hair who sat on the far side of Rupert drew his attention to Lucy's presence.

He turned, pushed his chair back and smiled, holding out an arm and beckoning.

'Hey, everyone, this is Lucy. Come and join us. I've told everyone about you.'

After a chorus of hellos she sat at the only free seat, at one end of the table. A profusion of dishes, almost more than the table could hold, lay before her.

Rupert had been busy.

'Where's the famous goat's cheese-and-walnut salad you promised me?' she asked, teasing.

A middle-aged man with a long, untidy beard passed a bowl.

'Here you are. I prefer the beetroot and, er, green stuff,' he explained, waving to another bowl.

The others all jumped in with their own preferred dishes, encouraging her to taste them and drawing Lucy into their banter.

Rupert's food was a huge success and, as she slipped the first forkful into her mouth, she understood why.

Her eyes slid to his. He was watching her. A taste explosion hit her tongue and she closed her eyes in appreciation.

When she opened them again he was still watching. She kissed her fingers in appreciation of his food.

He grinned, winked and resumed his conversation with the man next to him, leaving her to enjoy the experience without the pressure of reacting to his unsettling presence.

So far she'd only sampled the salt-encrusted potatoes. What would the veggies and the cheese taste like?

'What do you think of it?' the woman on her left asked.

Lucy rolled her eyes.

'I've been trying to persuade Rupert to do takeaways. He'd make a fortune.'

'Yes, he should.' She turned towards their host. 'You should, Rupert.'

'Should what?'

'Do takeaway.'

He shot an amused look at Lucy.

'Oh, no. Been there, done that, not going back.'

'I probably couldn't afford it, anyway,' Lucy added with a sigh.

'I thought you were a vet,' someone said.

'Yes, but I have two mortgages and a vacant partner position.'

Plus a threatening letter from the bank she'd been trying to forget about. Her stiff upper lip started to wobble.

'Isn't there anyone to help?' the man with the beard asked.

She shook her head and focused on her food. She was far too close to unloading all the negativity that had bubbled back to the surface after a couple of weeks of positive thinking.

She couldn't do that before strangers. She had come here to forget her woes, not weep into her food and make everyone uncomfortable!

Still, the question had thrust her financial crisis back into her mind. She could solve it by selling her third share of the surgery to Jamie and his mum but that would mean relinquishing control.

They could decide to sell up, leaving Lucy looking for new premises — or a new job!

The vets in Bickerston had vaguely mooted merging practices some months back but she dreaded being swallowed by the much bigger practice and becoming just an employee with little say.

Rupert's voice could be heard, bright and cheerful, describing a mound they would build that afternoon. It shifted the conversation away from her.

From a glance they shared she knew he had done it deliberately. Silently she thanked him and kept her head down for the rest of the meal.

The Quail's Box

'First we dig out a pit about a foot deep,' Rupert explained. 'Then we put on a thick layer of wood, cover it with leaves and compost and, finally, top with soil and turf.

'And there you have it! A raised bed that requires no digging or fertilising for ten or twenty years.'

Digging and filling the Hügel mound provided a distraction from Lucy's problems and the physical labour gave her a buzz.

Her mobile rang once — a cat owner asking for advice on a pet she'd treated earlier that week. She would pay for this peace and quiet later when she was trying to sleep, she knew.

For now, she was enjoying it.

Late afternoon Rupert pointed to a runner making his way up the path at the edge of the field. It was Michael.

He waved as he passed by.

'That's your special constable friend,

I think. He's not spying on you, is he?'

The edge to Rupert's voice did not match his amused expression.

Lucy recalled that, not so long ago, she'd wondered the same thing.

'He's training for an ultramarathon.'

'He doesn't like me,' Rupert commented.

'He thinks you could be the thief.'

'Really?'

'I didn't say I agreed with him.'

'Where am I keeping the stolen animals?' he asked, his arms stretched wide.

'That's what I said.' she told him.

Rupert looked thoughtful.

'Don't you find it odd that the first time he comes to ask me about the thefts is when you're here?'

'Odd? In what way?'

Rupert gave her a look.

'He's in love with you, Lucy. He might have planned to speak to me about Uncle Fester at some point but it's no coincidence he arrived when you were here.

'Plus, I spend a lot of time outside but I've never seen him run past before. He could be spying on you. On us, even.'

Lucy remembered the conversations she'd had with Michael about Rupert.

'You think he's jealous? But there's no need! You and I are friends.'

'Did you tell him so?'

Lucy nodded.

'Perhaps he thinks we're in collusion,' she jested. 'Cash-strapped professional teams up with the new face in town!'

He laughed and she changed the subject.

'My dad would be interested in what you're doing here. Did you arrange to meet him yet?'

'We've gone from 'no-one to be jealous of' to 'meeting the family' already?'

She looked at him sharply. He was grinning. Then his expression changed.

'Sorry. Yes, thank you. He rang and I told him to call round any time.'

When they'd finished building the mound Rupert suggested a comfort break.

'Come and see Alison,' he invited Lucy. 'She's broody! She's in the duck stall.'

Lucy followed him into the stables. The little grey Indian runner duck was sitting by herself in a nest box made from a plastic container laid on its side.

Her beak was tucked in and she opened a beady eye as they stepped inside.

But Lucy's eyes were not on Alison as Rupert explained how thrilled he was to raise ducklings the natural way without messing around with incubators.

She was staring at a box in a far corner.

Eventually Rupert noticed.

'What is it?'

'Where did that box come from?' She pointed.

He looked puzzled.

'I don't know. It wasn't there earlier. Why?'

'That box is the one I brought the quail in. The one that vanished.'

Rupert's face blanched.

'How can you be sure?'

'I took it to my dad's from the clinic.' She went to it and snatched it up.

'See this logo? It's a well-known supplier of veterinary medicines.

'And here.' She turned it around. 'The remains of an address label. You can just see the end of my postcode.'

Rupert was speechless, turning the box from side to side.

She wanted to believe he had not disposed of the birds and kept the box, but the suspicions Michael had raised returned to her.

'You know nothing about him, Lucy. Are you sure he's not attention-seeking?'

It was true. She knew hardly anything about Rupert. And wasn't it a fact that con men were often charming and charismatic, the last people to lie to you?

Was Rupert lying to her?

'Lucy, that box wasn't here this morning when I let the ducks out, I swear.'

He sounded sincere. If he was acting this was an Oscar-winning performance.

'I want to believe you, Rupert. I do.'

But hadn't she learned the hard way not to trust anyone?

'I love you, Lucy, and want us to be together for ever. Marry me.'

She shook memories of Jamie out of

her head. He was the past, a painful lesson to be put behind her.

'You must see how it looks,' she replied, wrapping her arms around her body.

Rupert nodded, despair showing in his eyes.

'Someone else put it there. They must have! I'll ask the others; maybe one of them found it.'

He turned and strode out of the shed, his usual air of calm confidence replaced by desperate determination.

Lucy stared after him, wanting to believe him but knowing she couldn't take his word blindly.

This meant that she couldn't trust him and, for her self-preservation, she would need to distance herself from him.

Her life was too complicated to risk getting hurt again right now.

Her phone rang. A farmer suspected pneumonia in a prostrate calf.

Normality restored, Lucy hurried to her car and drove away from Longmeadow without looking back.

A Chat with Jack

For the rest of the weekend Rupert's mood cast a damper on the atmosphere. The volunteers questioned him. Was he OK? Had they done something wrong?

He reassured them and asked if anyone could explain the presence of the box without telling them its significance.

None could.

After they left on Sunday evening he wandered along the new path in his 'forest garden', mulling over the event.

The only reason someone would plant the box would be to implicate him. Michael?

The man suspected him and had been around Longmeadow that afternoon. But he worked for the police, which should place him above suspicion.

Who else could it be? Lucy? Only a deranged person would bring a present, steal it and plant damning evidence later. What would she gain?

Although, now he thought about it, he

only had her word for it that it was this box that had contained the quail. Also, Michael was in love with her and likely to believe everything she said.

Was she seeking attention? Or was Lucy so broke she'd resort to stealing animals to sell, then frame someone else for it?

Did she hold a grudge against Rupert? She'd wanted to buy Longmeadow in the past. Perhaps she resented him being here.

No, instinct told him it was not Lucy.

That left an unknown person.

Rupert breathed in deeply and let it out in a whoosh. To clear himself from suspicion, he would have to uncover the truth.

If Lucy believed him guilty he'd never see her again. He wanted her at his table again, enjoying his food, looking happy and relaxed.

There had been such a positive difference in her recently and he believed it was, in part, down to him.

He couldn't throw that away and

watch her return to her stressed and overworked former self.

With his hands balled into fists he turned for the house.

First, he rang the police.

They explained it would take several days for someone — Michael, most likely — to attend.

Next, he wrote a list of local people and what he knew about them. The list was brief and the facts briefer.

Frustrated, he decided to pay a visit to his nearest neighbour, Jack Turner.

'I just wondered how you are, after Uncle Fester went missing and then those geese turning up,' Rupert began after the usual introductions. 'It must have been a shock for you.'

'All part of the ups and downs of farming life,' Jack replied philosophically.

He remained in the doorway of his house, neither inviting Rupert in nor stepping outside to join him. Chatty but not friendly, then.

'At least the insurance company coughed up for me horse,' Jack added.

'They didn't quibble because of the crime wave.'

'Still,' Rupert sympathised, 'it doesn't compensate for the stress, does it?'

'You're right there, lad. That horse would've fetched four thousand at market. Good stock, he came from.'

Rupert whistled astonishment at the price while wondering if Lucy knew about Jack's payout. Didn't she say Jack owed her money?

'I lost some quail myself,' he said.

The farmer nodded.

'Bit cheeky, that, in daylight.'

'Any idea who's behind it all?'

Jack's expression grew wary.

'There are rumours some fancy you for it.'

Rupert shook his head.

'Not guilty. I wouldn't know how to lead a horse into a box or where to put it if I succeeded! To be honest, big animals like that scare me.'

'You might have an accomplice, though.'

Rupert laughed.

137

'They'd have to come from London to help. I'm still a stranger here — most people consider me a fruit cake, what with my new-age ideas.'

Jack nodded, though whether he agreed with Rupert's assessment of the locals or their assessment of Rupert wasn't clear.

'Nowt wrong with new ideas if they work,' he pronounced. 'Farming must move on, else we'd still plough with oxen and let the stock die of scrofula.'

He began a long reminiscence about his childhood, growing up on a farm outside Lancaster.

Rupert let him talk because he liked to listen and he needed friends. However, he learned nothing new.

After leaving he texted Lucy.

Jack Turner tells me he received his insurance money.

There was no reply, which didn't surprise him. In Lucy's position he probably wouldn't respond, either.

Stolen Property

On Wednesday Michael appeared at Longmeadow.

Rupert would have preferred another officer but accepted a member of the rural crimes team was appropriate.

He showed Michael the box, explained how it had turned up and repeated the story of the quail's disappearance.

'So? What do you think?'

Michael remained silent for half a minute, his mouth intermittently twitching in thought. His eyes scanned the stables.

'There is only one obvious explanation,' he said finally. 'That you 'stole' your own property.'

Anger surged through Rupert, gathering in his stomach and sweeping up into his chest and neck. His temples throbbed.

'Didn't you hear a word I said? I did not do this!'

'I heard you. But nothing else makes sense.'

'What about you? How about maybe you're jealous of my friendship with Lucy?

'Perhaps you sneaked in while we were busy, took the birds and then dropped the box off on Saturday while on your run.'

Rupert jabbed an angry finger at the special constable who stepped back and held out his arm, palm facing Rupert.

'I must ask you to keep calm, sir.'

Rupert retreated and forced his anger into abeyance. Behaving aggressively towards the police would not help.

'Right, I'm calm. But what do you say to my obvious explanation?'

'That it's ridiculous.'

'Do you deny having feelings for Lucy?'

'I didn't say that.'

'You didn't have to. It's obvious. You don't want anyone coming between you, do you?'

Michael tried to turn the conversation again.

'This isn't about me or Lucy. This is about criminal activity.'

'That's not down to me, either.'

Rupert spun around, arms outstretched.

'Where am I hiding these animals? Longmeadow has two fields, a garden and three outhouses. You're welcome to search them all.'

Michael hesitated. Rupert assumed he would decline the offer but eventually he nodded.

'As long as I have your permission. I must warn you we've received information that there is evidence here to prove you guilty.'

Rupert stared at him, looking for signs he was joking. He saw none.

'Who from?'

Michael's expression remained inscrutable.

'I'm not at liberty to disclose that, sir.'

Rupert stared in disbelief, then led Michael towards the outhouses, clenching and unclenching his fists as he walked.

He must stay calm. It was in his interests to cooperate and clear his name.

Fortunately he'd checked beforehand for any incriminating objects.

An ear from a Tamworth boar, complete with identification tag, propped against the kitchen door, for example!

When they'd finished Rupert sighed. 'Satisfied?'

'You'd hardly leave evidence lying around when you knew I was coming.'

'That's the first sensible thing you've said.' Rupert pointed to the box. 'Similarly, I'd hardly leave that lying about when Lucy was coming and take her to where it sat!'

Michael turned towards his car.

'I'll write a report.'

'Aren't you going to take the box as evidence?'

'Why?'

'Fingerprints! And anything else forensics might turn up. I hear they can work miracles now.'

Michael snorted.

'For major crime, yes. Not for something like this. Besides, there will be many fingerprints on there — everyone at the vet supply company, the delivery man, Lucy, her employees and Basil.'

'Basil? You mean Lucy's dad?'

Michael nodded.

'Even if we find useful prints they will belong to someone who touched it legitimately, which includes you.'

Rupert stared, his heart plummeting. The casual way Michael used Lucy's dad's name reminded Rupert he was still very much the incomer. The locals shared a common past which he did not.

But why was one of them picking on him? What had he done wrong?

Michael headed back to his car, pausing at the Chetwynd rubbish bin at the roadside. The lid was slightly ajar.

He opened the lid and peered inside. Then he pulled out a pen and, using it, lifted out some leather straps.

Rupert's heart thumped alarmingly. What was this?

'What is it?'

Michael eyed him coolly.

'A halter for a horse you don't own.'

Beware of the Duck

'Evening, Alison. I hope you're keeping those eggs nice and toasty.'

His broody duck eyed him suspiciously.

'You're bringing up the next generation,' Rupert continued, sweeping the floor free of soiled wood shavings ready to hose down the concrete beneath. 'It's a lot of responsibility, old girl. Your babies are relying on you.

'The only thing I've raised is bread dough! I haven't brought up children.' He stopped sweeping, leaned on his brush and stared into the distance. 'And I never will now.

'Still, that's better for the planet. Too many people are wrecking it for you animals.' He recommenced sweeping. 'I'll work hard to build a better world for your babies. How about that?'

Alison growled as his brush came close to her nest and Rupert jumped. He'd never heard that noise before.

He edged closer and she growled again.

Was she ill? In pain? Suffering some metabolic disturbance? She'd eaten and drunk little since turning broody.

Lucy would know but she wasn't returning his texts and news of the horse harness would have reached her by now.

Nevertheless, Lucy wouldn't ignore a sick patient, whatever her opinion of its owner.

He pulled out his phone and texted.

Alison growls when I go near her. Should I worry?

He sighed and resumed leaning on his broom. Alison resumed peering suspiciously. They eyed each other briefly.

'Who took the quail, Alison?'

He'd pondered this all week along with if Lucy would ever speak to him again. He had hoped she'd keep him company on his stall at the farmer's market tomorrow.

Not that he'd make it there now without a lift. The police had taken his car.

His phone beeped — Lucy.

His hopes rose. He clicked on the text.

Broody ducks growl in warning. Stay back.

No hint of a personal message. It was entirely professional.

Thanks. That's a weight off my mind.

He put the phone back in his pocket and threw himself into hard work.

★ ★ ★

Lucy dropped her phone into her bag.

'Work,' she told Michael, not wishing to admit Rupert knew her mobile number.

Michael made a show of checking his watch but said nothing.

After Jamie left she and Michael had started meeting once a week for a drink at the Red Lion. Recently they had met less often, though.

Being in training, Michael stuck to soft drinks. Lucy, whose world was continuing to unravel, picked up her glass of red wine.

'I still can't believe he'd do something

like that,' she said, staring bleakly ahead.

'The duck chap?'

'Don't call him that. He has a name.'

'Sorry,' Michael soothed but added, 'we'll get fingerprints off the harness. You know he drives a silver four-by-four, don't you?'

Lucy sipped her wine.

'Half the village drives them. Including me, Rupert, Jack Turner and my father. You need a number plate or forensic evidence from inside the car.'

Michael stared into his orange juice.

'We're working on that.'

Lucy goggled at him.

'You've taken Rupert's car?'

Michael nodded.

'We received a tip-off. And after finding the harness, well, if he used it to transport any stolen animals we'll find the evidence.'

Lucy struggled to process this information.

'But how could he take a pig or a horse? He has no trailer,' she reasoned aloud. 'Aren't you overreacting?'

'As far as we know he owns no trailer. We're looking at garage rentals, etc.'

Lucy slammed her glass down.

'You're convinced he did it, aren't you?'

'He's our only suspect. He's intelligent. He wouldn't keep incriminating items at the smallholding.'

'Then why would he keep the box?' Michael shrugged.

'Maybe he thought it too generic to be noticed. A box is a box.'

True, but Lucy would recognise one of her own supply boxes. Rupert would see that.

'Just when I decide to start trusting someone this happens,' she muttered.

Michael caught her hand in his.

'You can trust me, Lucy.'

She squeezed his hand briefly before letting go. Right now she needed to keep everyone at a safe distance.

'I want to, Michael. But after Jamie and now Rupert, even you have no chance.'

Michael frowned, then reached for his phone.

'This will cheer you up.'

He would be searching the internet for a funny video. It was just what she needed.

That, and Rupert to be innocent.

Lodger Wanted

Lucy entered the village shop to do the unthinkable.

'Have you got a card?' she asked Josie. 'I want to put up an ad.'

Josie handed her one from a box.

'What are you advertising?'

'Room to rent.' Lucy focused on the card, avoiding eye contact.

'I heard you'd been asking around for a lodger,' Josie said. 'Feeling lonely in the evenings or do you need the rent?'

It was definitely the rent.

'Bit of both,' Lucy said briefly.

'Bit of a shock when him from Longmeadow got arrested,' Josie continued. 'You're very friendly with him by all accounts.'

'He keeps animals,' Lucy reminded her. 'And he was interviewed, not arrested.'

This did nothing to stop Josie's flow.

'Very hot chef, too. Weren't you helping him with pies for his stall?'

Lucy wondered how such information leaked out.

'Yes, he asked for my opinion. He's still making friends and spends a lot of time setting up his smallholding.'

'He had a load of people over at the weekend, I heard. They buried something in the garden,' Josie said pointedly.

Lucy counted to ten.

'It wasn't carcasses, Josie, just bits of wood to add compost to the soil.'

'Is that right? Still, a bit odd, isn't it? That's not what Esme Wilberforce did when she owned Longmeadow.'

Secretly Lucy found the Hügel mound weird, too, but it would certainly sequester carbon from the saplings Rupert had removed from the garden.

Burning them would have added to greenhouse gases. So that made sense.

She concentrated on writing her card and marvelled on the way she'd shifted from avoiding Rupert to defending him.

'Esme never buried stuff,' Josie continued. 'I hear he's been begging manure from all over.'

'Which suggests he hasn't got his own horses and pigs making it, doesn't it?'

Lucy finished writing and handed Josie the card. The shopkeeper read it.

'Mates rates for you, love. Two-fifty.'

Once Lucy had paid Josie bustled over to the ad display, took a card from the centre and replaced it with Lucy's.

'There. People should see that. We don't want our vet going under, do we?'

Lucy silently apologised to the dog-walker whose ad had been demoted to bottom left. Her cheeks were flushed.

Advertising her financial difficulties like this was so embarrassing.

'Did you hear?' Josie added as Lucy went to leave. 'Jack Turner had his insurance money through.

'He's buying another horse with it so if he owes you money stake a claim quick!'

Lucy walked back to the car digesting this latest piece of news. She knew about the cheque via Rupert but not Jack's intention to replace Uncle Fester.

Why would he do that? He already owned a stud stallion — Tonto, Uncle

Fester's sire.

Lucy popped back into the shop.

'Why is Jack buying another horse?'

'Well, you know Tonto got struck by lightning a couple of months back?'

Lucy shook her head.

'You might have been away that week.'

Lucy nodded. She'd attended a two-day update for treating large animals.

'Then why . . . ?' Lucy's voice faded as she thought the problem through.

'Not my business,' Josie said, though clearly she thought it was and was miffed she didn't know the answer.

A Lame Stallion

Outside Jack Turner's house a new black SUV stood in place of his old silver one, Lucy saw as she drove up. She hoped he hadn't spent all his money already.

Jack's wife answered the door. She removed her glasses on a string and let them dangle.

'Hello, Lucy. Did Jack call? He didn't mention it.'

Lucy shook her head.

'This is an impromptu visit about his bill. It's getting quite large and very urgent.'

She let the implication hover, hoping Mrs Turner, if not Jack, would grasp it and feel obliged to pay.

Instead the woman developed a guarded look.

'You'll have to speak to Jack about that. He handles the farm finances.'

'Does he?' Lucy asked doubtfully. 'I thought one of your subjects at the tech was accounting software.'

'That's my work, not Jack's.'

Lucy's lips tightened.

'Josie Grainger tells me he's bought a replacement stallion.'

'Not yet. He's looking, though. You heard about Tonto?'

Lucy nodded. Assuming Jack had received insurance money for him, as well, he should have cash to spare. Unless all of it had gone on that new car.

'It made me wonder why he was selling Uncle Fester.'

Mrs Turner examined her fingernails.

'I expect he wants new blood.'

That made sense. Jack wouldn't breed from a stallion and mare that were close blood relatives.

'I think he said he was checking a fence in the bottom field,' Mrs Turner said. 'If you want to speak to him.'

The bottom field was a 10-minute walk away.

'Could you phone him to check?'

'Doesn't keep his phone on him when he's on the farm,' his wife replied, her arms crossed.

Was that true? Lucy raised a suspicious eyebrow.

She suspected this would be a wild goose chase but set off in search of Jack anyway.

Twenty minutes of trudging about the farm yielded nothing more substantial than a whiff of aftershave.

No doubt Mrs Turner had tipped him off as soon as Lucy was out of sight — assuming Jack hadn't been indoors all along.

Eventually Lucy admitted defeat and trudged back to her car. From pure frustration she texted him.

Pay at least half your outstanding bill within seven days or face me in the small claims court.

That was what she should have done ages ago.

She hit *send* and threw the phone on to the passenger seat, for once not caring what anyone thought of her.

With the thrill of achievement rushing around her body she put the car in gear and spat dust behind her as she accelerated down the long drive.

Five minutes later she arrived at the next farm for a follow-up visit on a horse suffering from cellulitis, a serious skin infection.

She watched the horse as Judith, the owner, led it around the yard. She could see no sign of lameness now.

She ran her hand over the animal's fetlock, the centre of the infection, and found virtually no residual swelling or warmth. Good.

'He's responded well,' Lucy said. 'I'll give him one last antibiotic injection to ensure the infection doesn't recur.'

While drawing up the injection she decided to fish for information.

'I've just come from Jack Turner's. A bit of bad luck, what happened to his stallion, Tonto.

'I was away — I only just found out.'

Judith crossed her arms.

'Bit of luck, if you ask me. He was going lame.'

'Oh?'

'He was stumbling a bit. Apparently,'

Judith added as though in afterthought. 'And then losing Uncle Fester, too.'

'He has suffered unusual bad luck.'

Judith said this flatly, suggesting there was more to the story than she was letting on.

But she wouldn't be drawn further, and Lucy drove away with more questions than answers.

★ ★ ★

That night she arrived home, tired, to an empty house. She opened the fridge for a pizza and saw the space where Jamie's beer used to be.

She slammed the door and turned to light the oven. Her oven gloves sprawled over the hob. Jamie would have tidied them on to their designated hook.

In the living-room the handset from his games console was not lying on the coffee table. Everywhere she looked reminded her of her loss and an American marine biologist's gain.

Lucy burst into tears. Without Jamie

the house was a soulless box. Why had she been looking on it as her castle?

After work she missed having someone to hold. To sink into their arms and say nothing because you didn't have to.

She missed inconsequential chatter over a cup of tea or glass of wine, light-hearted bickering over the TV remote. And yes, she missed having someone to unload to.

Tonight, she needed to talk.

Maybe a lodger wouldn't be so bad, after all.

She sniffed back the tears and filled a glass from a half-drunk bottle of Merlot. Who could she call, to chat about anything except work?

She tried her dad. He would tell her about his birds or his U3A classes. But he didn't answer and she left a message.

She tried Michael next but the call went straight through to voicemail. Probably he was out training.

Lucy's sister, an eight-hour time difference away, would just be starting work. Closer to home, her female friends would be sitting down to tea with their families.

Her thoughts turned to Rupert whose words rang clear in her memory.

'Any time you need to unload.'

Her fingers itched to phone him.

She could almost feel his strong and capable arms about her, remembering the embrace they'd shared after the quail disappeared.

A moment of togetherness. A fraternal, uncomplicated, unconditional, caring embrace. She'd sensed in that moment she would always be safe with Rupert.

The memory warmed her. She had felt right in his arms, as though that was where she was meant to be.

Tomorrow was market day again. Lucy wasn't on call and she had previously considered dropping by to see if he needed help, always hoping that he did.

That was until she had found the incriminating box.

She threw her phone on to the sofa and picked up the remote control instead.

'Piffle and rot,' she muttered and turned on the TV.

She would find something else to do tomorrow — something for herself.

If Rupert had taught her anything it was to make more 'me' time.

Inspiration

Sleep had come easily, with pleasant dreams of red-speckled lettuce leaves and of developing a satisfying glow from digging her own Hügel mound.

Lucy awoke, refreshed, with a whole different attitude to her neglected back garden. It should provide pleasure, not represent outdoor housework.

Over breakfast she gazed out at it. On the lengthening lawn buttercups shone in the early rays of another scorching day.

Purple flowers with pretty cream bells bobbed in the breeze. Daisies nestled like small white pennies on the ground. Bees buzzed about them all.

How beautiful it promised to be, with a little work. How useful — and relaxing, too. Not cutting the grass, she now realised, created a better space for wildlife.

Rupert would be delighted.

Lucy shook that idea away. His opinion was no concern of hers.

Today began her garden makeover. Where stood boring low-maintenance shrubs she'd plant rhubarb and gooseberry bushes and sow a bed of salad leaves next to the shed.

A small greenhouse would fit in the top corner, when she could afford one.

She retrieved a hand trowel and kneeling pad from the tiny shed, then wondered where to start. The lawn?

Optimistic Lucy wanted to dig up the lawn — Rupert didn't waste good soil on something he couldn't eat. Practical Lucy shuddered. What on earth would she plant in all that extra space?

'Besides,' she said to herself as a bee bumbled past, 'since I stopped cutting it it's become a wildlife meadow.'

She started by weeding unwanted plants from between shrubs.

Two hours later, limbs aching, she sipped iced tea at the café table on the patio. She had created several inviting bare patches of soil already and more would follow.

Meanwhile, she needed inspiration

and the garden centre was the place to find it.

Rupert's advice to buy lettuce seed and throw them in the ground sounded too simple, particularly if she wanted a mixture of leaves like he had.

She should take someone more experienced to the garden centre, to be certain of buying the right seeds.

Rupert was off-limits because he might be cheating by nature as well as by name. Also, he'd be busy at the farmer's market.

Her father? She'd been neglecting him lately. The previous evening she had promised to ring him today.

Grinning, she grabbed her mobile.

'Hi,' she said when he answered.

'Sorry, who is this?' he replied, joking.

'The person who's going to buy you red velvet cake from an award-winning café.'

'I'm listening, whoever you are.'

Lucy laughed.

'Listen, why don't we head to Gardener's Delight? I want to plant something.'

'Can't your boyfriend come out to play?'

His choice of words shocked Lucy.

'What boyfriend?'

'Rupert Chetwynd. According to Josie you've practically moved in.'

Lucy suspected he was grinning.

'You know the police think he's the animal rustler, don't you?'

'What happened to innocent until proven guilty?' he retorted. 'Anyway, you've sold me on red velvet cake. By the time you arrive I might even have my shoes on.'

Lucy shook her head with amusement as she rang off. Her dad's grumbles about arthritis were exaggerated.

Dodgy hips and knees stopped him striding over the hills and manhandling sheep now, but he could touch his toes, still rose at seven and always looked smart.

Lucy's Way

Banks of bright flowers greeted them at the garden centre.

'These are pretty.' Lucy gently lifted a purple flower. 'What are they?'

'Geraniums? I'm not a flower person.'

'But the farm had a big cottage garden.'

'That was your mother's. If it doesn't have four legs or lay eggs I'm not interested.'

Lucy understood that. Her own interest in plants up to now had lain purely in their usefulness or threat to animals.

She and her father found a wide variety of lettuce seedlings that perplexed them both.

'Why don't you phone your new guru?' Basil suggested.

Guru was a better word than boyfriend, Lucy conceded, but she still wasn't going to phone Rupert for help.

'He'll be busy on his stall,' she said.

'He isn't.'

'You seem very sure.'

Her father squinted at something labelled 'Morton's mix'.

'I was at Longmeadow when you rang yesterday. I left my phone in the car, which is why I didn't answer at the time.'

'Oh.' This should not be a surprise — she'd put the two of them in contact.

But why hadn't she known about the meeting? Why hadn't either of them said?

Because she wasn't speaking to Rupert and she didn't ring her father often enough, that was why.

'Why isn't he at the market?'

'No transport. The police are still holding his car and he doesn't know anyone with a suitable vehicle to help.'

Her father looked at Lucy pointedly. Her car was big enough. Her father's was not.

'I thought you liked this man,' he continued.

'I do. I did.'

Did she want to discuss complex personal feelings with her dad right now?

She was supposed to be doing something completely different to forget and move on.

Lucy spotted the seed section.

'Come on, we can do this. Packets carry instructions. They'll be much easier than living plants.'

Her dad pursed his lips.

'You don't trust him, do you?'

'I don't know what you mean.'

Lucy peered at the instructions on a packet of 'Lattuga', which she suspected was Italian for lettuce, and wondered what a fine tilth was.

'Just because Michael suspects him, suddenly you won't talk to him. Not everyone's like Jamie, Lucy.'

'I know.' She put the Lattuga in her basket and picked up some Little Gem.

'Besides, Jamie wasn't as bad as you make out.'

Lucy stared at him.

'What do you mean? He lied to me! Not a little white lie but a great, big, whopping, life-changing one!'

'Did he, though? Really?'

'I don't know what you mean.'

'Hadn't he wanted to delay joining his dad, to see a bit more of the world first?'

Lucy cast her mind back.

'Well, yes, but Tony's senior partner had been eager to retire. Tony needed us.'

'As I recall, Jamie wasn't keen on the extension, either.'

'What are you saying? That him leaving was all my fault?'

Her father shook his head.

'No, love. I just think he might have had a different agenda to yours all along, but you just didn't see it.'

Lucy felt a vein throbbing in her temple. She thrust her chin out.

'He could have said no to the extension. Nobody forced him to sign.'

Her father looked at her and sighed.

'Look, all I'm saying is you need to trust someone again eventually. And to do that you need to listen to them. Really listen.

'Look beyond their words for the hidden agenda.'

'I trust you.' She added Little Gem to her basket. 'I listen to you. And I trust Elaine.'

Her father snorted with derision.

'You do not! You won't give her any autonomy. It's Lucy's way or no way!'

'What do you mean?'

'Elaine and I are both members of the bowls club.'

Lucy stared at him.

'Your hips let you bowl?'

'No, they let me prop up the bar where Elaine sits and tells me she's hitting a brick wall. You.'

Lucy's mouth opened and closed a few times and her father carried on.

'You've loosened up a little recently but you don't allow her the freedom Tony did.'

She focused on the seeds once more.

'She shouldn't discuss work with you.'

'She didn't disclose specifics, just some things she can't do now that she used to.'

Lucy realised she hadn't discussed quite a few things with Elaine since deciding to turn her life around, including the ultimatum she'd given Jack.

'Aren't the fingerprints back yet?'

The sudden change of subject threw her.

'What fingerprints?'

'The ones from the horse harness.'

'How do you know about those?'

Basil looked at her like she was mad.

'Everyone knows. And I was round there last night, don't forget.'

'Then he'd have told you if they were back,' she answered triumphantly.

'You think he'd know before Josie or you?'

'Why would I know first?' Lucy challenged.

'Because Michael would soon tell you if Rupert's prints are on there. If they aren't present the case against him is entirely circumstantial.

'Anyone could have dropped that halter in his bin, even Michael.'

'Michael wouldn't do that,' Lucy protested. 'I've known him —'

'About as long as you've known Jamie.'

She screwed her face into a frown. His point was valid.

Just because she'd known someone since childhood didn't mean they wouldn't lie to her. Michael had been acting oddly recently, and he'd lost his job.

Money must be tight.

Rumours

Pulling out her phone Lucy called Michael, who answered sounding out of breath.

'Just wondering if there's any news on the case,' she began casually.

'What case?'

'The one you interviewed Rupert Chetwynd for!' she said, frustrated.

'Interestingly, the thefts have stopped,' he told her.

Was he serious?

'It's been a couple of days, for heaven's sake! What about the fingerprints?'

'I can't divulge that information,' he said flatly.

'The results are back?'

'Apparently.'

'But you won't tell me whose they were.'

No answer. Lucy wondered what she could ask that might shed light on Rupert's predicament. None came to mind.

She changed tack.

'Have you heard any rumours about Jack Turner's horses?'

'What about them?'

'One struck by lightning after he began stumbling and Uncle Fester's insurance money going towards a new stud.'

'Won't he just want fresh bloodstock?'

Probably, Lucy thought, but went on.

'Seems coincidental. And Uncle Fester is larger than the other stolen livestock.

'Mostly the thieves took small animals easy to transport and sell on like my dad's birds. Even if you find them, you can't prove they're his.

'Horses are tricky, though, especially now they're micro-chipped. I put Uncle Fester's chip in myself.'

It was one of Jack's outstanding bills.

'To sell him you'd need to replace the chip and fake a new passport.

Lucy was thinking aloud.

'So Uncle Fester is the odd one out, not the quail.'

Michael sighed.

'I'll ask around,' he said, clearly

humouring her.

Lucy glanced at her father who was discussing the price of sheep with someone she didn't recognise.

She wanted to discuss her frustration but any meaningful discussion with him would result in one succinct phrase.

'Get a grip, Lucy.'

Her thoughts returned to Rupert and those six simple words.

'Any time you need to unload.'

'He's one to watch for,' her father's voice broke into her reverie. The person he'd been talking to had gone.

Lucy's attention snapped back to him.

'Who?'

'Jack Turner. Wallet full of cobwebs, that man has.'

'Farming's going through lean times,' she offered.

Her father laughed.

'Jack's not a farmer. He's a horse breeder with a sharp eye on the bottom line.

'Haven't you noticed this year's top-of-the-range car gleaming on his drive?

He got it for a bargain, mind. He's a shrewd negotiator.

'Ask Tony about his horses, too.' Basil frowned. 'Except you can't, poor devil.'

'What about his horses?' Lucy prompted before her father started reminiscing about her old boss and the anecdotes they'd shared over lambing.

'It might be nothing but I heard that Tony was worried about Uncle Fester's grandsire. He was called out to him about lameness and wasn't happy.'

A firework went off in Lucy's brain. Of course!

Why hadn't she checked? North Millton vets had been treating Jack Turner's horses for decades.

'Shall we go pay for this lot?' she suggested brightly, heading for the checkouts.

Her father caught her arm.

'Not so fast, missy. You promised me cake!'

He spun her around to face the café.

'Don't worry, it's my treat. No arguments.'

Lucy opened her mouth, then shut it and smiled instead.

'OK, but only if you come home and advise on my garden. I'm clueless!'

Her father joined the short queue at the self-service counter and helped himself to red velvet cake.

'You think I'd have any more idea?'

Lucy chose a slice of carrot cake.

'Two heads are better than one.'

'We might make twice the mess!' Her father ordered two coffees. 'You should ask Organic Rupert to come over and help.'

'Do you think he's guilty?'

'What I think shouldn't matter, although he struck me as hard-working, principled and honest.'

Her father was usually an excellent judge of character. Maybe she should give 'Organic Rupert' the benefit of the doubt.

She smiled at the new epithet and hauled out her phone again. If nothing else, he'd know what a fine tilth was.

Have you received the fingerprint results?

she texted.

The reply came quickly for a man she assumed was working hard on his patch.

No. Should I?

Michael says they're back.

Her phone rang and it was Rupert. Lucy picked up.

'So?' he asked before she could speak. 'Whose did they find?'

'I don't know. I assumed you would.'

She hoped they would prove he was not the thief. She wanted him to be innocent so they could renew and grow their friendship.

If he was guilty it would reinforce her view that men were untrustworthy!

'Oh.' His deflation was almost palpable. 'I guess I should ring the station.'

'I guess. Will you let me know?'

Rupert laughed nervously.

'If the cops let me speak to anyone ever again.' With that he cut the call.

Lucy realised her father was still present, had finished his cake and was watching her.

'Anyone I know?'

She forked a large piece of carrot cake. 'Organic Rupert.'

'You know it only proves anything if his prints are on the halter, don't you?'

Whose Prints?

After she arrived home Lucy received another text.

Prints but not mine!

Relief coursed through Lucy, yet she dithered about phoning him. Why?

Perhaps because her father was right — absence of evidence did not prove innocence. And because the memory of finding her box in his stables still lingered.

But her dad was also correct in that she needed to trust people more; at least, the right people. Rupert seemed the right sort of person.

The desire for his company and help in the garden overcame reticence and suspicion. They'd be gardening, not setting up home together. If he agreed to help.

'Hi.' Rupert sounded wary when he answered.

'You can't not tell me!' Lucy cried eagerly. 'Whose prints were they?'

'I don't know.'

'They wouldn't tell you?'

'Nope. They said it's confidential information. I'm just relieved to be exonerated.

'Not that I have been, exactly. The police still think I did it, though Lord knows how without a horsebox or any place to keep the dratted animal.

'To be honest, I'm a bit afraid of horses. They're so big and snorty!'

Lucy laughed. It was relief, she supposed, plus the absurdity of a man living his dream life in the country despite fearing some of the animals there.

'I hear you didn't make it to the market today,' she told him. 'What a shame.'

'The police still have my car.'

'Oh, yes, my father told me this morning. I forgot. I . . .'

She what? Wished she'd known because she'd have given him a lift? It wasn't true.

'I'll get it back soon.' He sounded resigned. 'I did persuade Josie Grainger to take duck eggs for the community shop and some tarts. Obviously it's early days but, so far, they're selling well.'

Lucy suddenly realised where she might find the answer to whose finger-prints were on the halter.

'Your cooking will be a fabulous addition to her range of fresh food,' she told him, then hesitated.

After the coldness she'd shown him over the last week she wouldn't blame him for refusing what she was about to ask.

'What are you doing today?' she began, to test the water.

'The usual. A bit of weeding, a bit of cooking, a bit of sowing.

'Actually, I should paint one of the spare bedrooms but it's far too nice to be indoors.'

Lucy agreed. It was one of those hot but breezy days where you could spend all day outdoors and not feel too warm, but could also end up horribly sun-burned if you weren't careful.

'You sound very busy,' she acknowl-edged.

'Why do you ask?'

'You've inspired me to grow something, only I'm clueless. Dad and I bought some seeds but, well, I need to go to Josie's shop anyway.

'I wondered, if I were to pick you up, would you mind being my Alan Titchmarsh?'

There was the briefest of pauses.

'You want me to do a garden makeover?' he asked incredulously.

'No, I just need advice, that's all. I'll do the work.'

Lucy held her breath for what seemed an age before Rupert replied.

'I would be honoured.'

Why are You Here?

Half an hour later Rupert arrived at Lucy's house on his bike. He had said he didn't want her driving out of her way.

In truth he needed the emotional space and freedom to leave when he wanted to under his own steam.

Her house was a modern brick semi in a cul-de-sac abutting farmland, a far stretch from Longmeadow. But warmer, he thought. The thick stone walls at Longmeadow took for ever to heat.

Her Subaru stood on the block paving drive. She opened the front door before he could ring the bell.

She looked flustered.

'Hi. Thanks for coming. I wouldn't blame you for telling me to take a hike after the way I cold-shouldered you this week.'

'You had your reasons,' he replied, though he didn't entirely understand them. 'Besides, I can never resist a damsel in distress.'

'Bring your bike around the back. I think we both learned the lesson that it's dangerous to leave anything portable out the front!'

She led him through a side gate into a conventional, rather unloved back garden.

A rectangle of overlong grass was surrounded on three sides by unkempt borders and on the fourth, next to the house, by a long thin patio.

It felt strange to be at Lucy's home for the first time, particularly after a week where she had not returned his texts.

As Rupert stowed his bike safely, balanced his helmet on top and changed out of his cycling shoes he told himself this meant nothing other than that she wanted to rekindle their budding friendship and she needed his expertise.

Not that he was an expert.

'Apparently they were Jack Turner's,' Lucy said.

Rupert stopped what he was doing to try to make sense of her statement.

'What were?'

'The fingerprints.'

'Ah. Well, that's unsurprising, considering it was his harness. Who was it who told you?'

Lucy laughed.

'Josie.'

Rupert turned towards her, his mouth forming an 'O' of astonishment.

'You're kidding!'

'Nope. Also I rang Michael and suggested that, if Jack's prints were on the harness, then he should be under suspicion.

'His reply was to ask why, as Jack's fingerprints were bound to be on it. Which confirms it.'

'Why do you suspect Jack?'

'Something my dad said about another of his horses. I need to do some research on the subject at the surgery but that can wait.

'I wanted to ask how you're feeling after everything.'

'Relieved,' he confessed. 'And confused. Worried, even.

'Why would someone try to implicate

me like that? What have I done wrong?'

'Nothing,' she assured him. 'I guess it's emotionally easier to implicate someone you don't know, someone you haven't lived alongside for ever.'

She moved to the café table on which she had left some plants and seed packets.

'As long as you've done nothing wrong it will all settle down. Wait and see.'

As long as you've done nothing wrong? She still doubted him, then.

'I haven't done anything wrong, Lucy,' he said.

Her expression changed. Her brow furrowed and her voice became less carefree, more earnest.

'I know you haven't. At least I think I know. I'm as sure as I can be . . .'

'I haven't,' he reiterated. 'I wouldn't.'

There was a pause before she spoke.

'May I ask something that's puzzling me?'

Rupert tensed but understood she still needed reassurance.

'What is it?'

187

'Why did you move to Lancashire? Why didn't you stay near friends and family where it would be much easier to make the connections you need for your new venture to thrive?'

Rupert's muscles unwound. That was an easy question to answer.

'Money, pure and simple. I could have bought the land I need down south but not a house the size of Longmeadow. The best I'd have managed down there was a tiny bungalow. Why?'

'It didn't make sense.' She shrugged. 'You're obviously missing your friends and family and it's making life harder for you.'

'You mean it's suspicious. Well, I'm not running away from a shady past, I can assure you.

'Longmeadow House is the perfect size for my volunteers. Eventually, I hope to run fully accredited permaculture courses, too.

'Delegates will need somewhere to stay and the bank was never going to give me a big mortgage, given my chosen lifestyle.'

Suddenly her demeanour changed from serious to bright, as though a line had been drawn under the subject.

'Anyway, we're here for my rubbish garden. What do you think of it?'

He ran assessing eyes over it, lingering on the flowering weeds.

'I'm pleased you're wildlife-friendly,' he said diplomatically.

'You're referring to my wildflower meadow, I gather.' She sucked in her cheeks.

Rupert laughed. They both knew her long grass, studded with nodding of yellow buttercups and orange fox-and-cubs had come about by omission, not design.

'People mow their lawns too often,' he responded. 'Not you, obviously. Now for the next stage.'

'This is what I bought.'

She showed him four packets of seeds and three courgettes bursting from their pots, then made a helpless gesture.

He examined the seeds.

'Good choices. A variety of salad leaves

and,' he added with a look of overdone admiration, 'radishes are always a winner.'

'I remember growing them for a school project when I was about six,' Lucy confessed.

Rupert walked her around the beds, discussing the pros and cons of what might go where.

He was enjoying focusing on the practical aspects of gardening and not the emotional implications of being here in Lucy's house.

They agreed on where to plant the courgettes and found some perfect compost in a Dalek-style bin that Lucy had forgotten she owned.

'I've put nothing in it since Jamie left,' she admitted, her mood suddenly forlorn and her eyes sad.

'I lost interest in everything for a while. It was only work which got me out of bed in the morning.'

His heart twisted with the pain of her loss. He laid his hand gently on her shoulder.

'Break ups are hard. I know from experience. But we're both still here, breathing and smiling!

'It's important to focus your energies on what's to come, not what's past.

'Let's sow the seeds of a positive future, shall we?' he added.

She gave a brave smile, then threw herself on him in a surprise hug.

Fortunately, it didn't last long and then she turned back to the garden.

White Feather

They shovelled compost into the ground beneath the courgettes then drew furrows, sowed the seeds and covered them up.

They labelled the rows then sat on the patio with sage tea, using the prunings from her herbs.

'It's good for your immune system and digestion, allegedly,' Rupert told her.

She blew on her cup and sipped.

'It's refreshing. And free. Elaine is always foisting herbal tea on me at work.

'Consider it an easy way to keep the plant in check. Instead of pruning it you just nip out for a few tea leaves every so often. It all comes down to how you think, really.

'And you must start using your compost bin again.'

Lucy looked horrified, no doubt remembering the huge cobwebs they'd found in there. She wouldn't go near it and had made him empty the whole thing.

'I thought you were an animal lover.'

'Animals, yes. Creepy crawlies, no!'

'So if someone brought in a tarantula?'

'I'd be totally professional,' Lucy answered with overdone sincerity, 'right up until the owner took the cover off the box and I ran screaming from the room!'

She grinned.

'I like sitting here,' Rupert told her. 'And I'm glad you called.'

Lucy bit her lip.

'I feel bad about walking away like I did. Jamie left me with serious trust issues.'

Rupert guessed it would be easy to have trust issues if your lifelong friend and soul mate failed to tell you what they really wanted to do with their life. Especially if they left you behind with massive debts.

'It did mean a lot that you rang,' he said. 'I miss the friends I left in London and I'd like us to be friends.'

He looked at her. The eye contact

lasted longer than it should for just friends. He should look away but didn't.

'I'd like that, too,' she replied. 'I enjoy your company. You remind me there are things in life beyond work and sleep.'

She broke off and looked away.

'Not that I got much sleep.'

'It's important to make 'me' time,' Rupert repeated.

Lucy's eyes wandered to the courgettes.

'And eat healthily. I was living on pizza.'

'Nothing wrong with pizza. Carbs, veg, dairy for calcium, a little protein. It's nearly a complete food!'

'Not a large deep crust with extra garlicky dough balls!'

'No, maybe not.'

'I'm trying to spend less on fresh sandwiches from Josie's shop, too, but they're so convenient and tastier than mine. It's a touch of luxury.'

Rupert thought finances really must be tight if she struggled to afford a sandwich.

'I'll give you lessons. You haven't tasted my cheese, watercress and pickles on sourdough, have you?'

He mentally checked his schedule for when he could fit this in — his watercress wasn't cropping yet.

'Sounds divine. How do I get my hands on your bread?'

'I'll show you how to make it. Sourdough is easy and takes little time. No kneading, and you can bung it in the fridge whenever you need to slow things down.'

Lucy's mouth fell open.

'I think I'm in love!'

Even though she was joking Rupert felt his stomach do a backflip. He struggled to keep his voice light.

'It's a date, then. Pick a weekend when you have all day and I'll give you a tutorial, free. Some bakers charge a fortune for sourdough classes!'

'You told me before that sourdough takes twenty-four hours to make.'

As he went to explain that, although the dough took a day to develop its flavour the amount of time spent working the dough was short, his phone trilled.

He glanced at it and frowned.

'It's the police. What do they want?'

'Maybe someone hasn't been informed you already know the fingerprint results?'

He hit the answer button.

'Hello, Rupert Chetwynd speaking.'

As the officer explained the reason for the call, Rupert's hopes for the future disintegrated all over again.

As the sergeant went on a pit of dread opened in his stomach and grew deeper and deeper.

He ended the call and stared at the phone in disbelief.

'What?' Lucy asked.

'I have to attend for more questioning. Now. I might be arrested.'

Lucy shrank into her chair.

'Why?'

Rupert swallowed, his voice desperate.

'They found a white goose feather in my car. They think I stole those geese.'

No Longer an Idyll

Lucy insisted on driving Rupert to Bickerston police station. He had wanted to cycle but she worried he would be too distracted to do so safely.

'Besides, what will they do with your bike? You could be there for . . .'

She stopped herself. It seemed unlikely that they'd keep him in the cells overnight. An animal thief was not a master criminal, and he had animals to tend.

'. . . ages,' she finished.

They removed most of her vet equipment and loaded his bike into her boot to take it to Longmeadow. She'd see to the ducks while she was there.

She let him out at the police station, a whirl of emotions running around her head and chest.

Her instinct still told her he was one of life's good guys — living an ecologically-sustainable life, caring for his animals.

But if the police had found a goose feather which had no reason to be in his car that might be difficult to explain.

Why would he steal livestock, though? And how had the geese got to Jack's via Lancaster?

Nothing made sense.

With a sinking feeling she watched him walk through the door. He didn't look back and his step had lost its usual spring. He looked like a man walking to the gallows.

Lucy remained curiously calm as she pulled away from the kerb and headed for Longmeadow House.

'You've done all you can,' she told herself. 'You gave him a solicitor's number and you're going to look after his ducks.'

She'd learned from her parents at an early age that there was little to be gained from worrying about things you could not influence, such as the weather.

While her heart might want to fret for him her head knew that was counterproductive and told her to get on with what needed to be done.

Longmeadow seemed lifeless without his cheerful smile and infectious enthusiasm. Lucy parked Rupert's bike in an empty part of the gloomy old stables then checked on Alison, hunkered down on her nest in a dark corner.

The duck had no inkling her owner might be facing jail, which meant she and her babies would need to move home.

Lucy shook that thought away and wondered instead when the ducklings were due. The grey Indian runner who reminded Rupert of his aunt had been sitting on her eggs for at least three weeks.

They took 28 days to hatch so hatching must be close.

She saw Rupert had built a barrier of boxes around the nest box to keep the ducklings contained and make sure Alison couldn't lead them out into the fields, where they would be in danger from crows and foxes and stray cats.

He cared. He was responsible.

'Oh, Alison,' she said aloud. 'Where will this end? My ambition has always been to be a vet in North Millton, to bring health and happiness to the pets and livestock of people I grew up with.

'Now my dreams are turning into nightmares! Your daddy's, too. He has such good ideas. He'd have made Longmeadow a great place for your babies to live.'

She stopped that train of thought, too. He probably would still make it a great place for her babies.

'I could have gone with Jamie, you know,' she told the duck. 'He asked me to, after he'd finally admitted the secret he'd been hiding all those years.

'He assumed I'd say yes but why should I give up the life I wanted to follow his dream? He'd lied to me once — he'd probably do it again.

'I don't want to live anywhere else. I like it here. And I like the people.'

Lucy stopped. Was that true? Over the last few months she'd learned North Millton wasn't the idyll she'd painted it to be.

It wasn't just Jamie who kept secrets; people she liked and trusted were taking advantage of her good nature.

They were lying to her and stealing.

Perhaps she should sell her stake in the surgery and move to where debt wasn't dragging her under for the third time.

Rupert had done so, after all. He'd left his problems behind to build a new life.

He'd reminded her of what she'd been missing since Jamie left. Fun, good food, relaxation. What it was like to be happy.

'Your dad makes me happy, Alison.'

The duck opened an eye and then closed it again when Lucy didn't move.

'Is there any point struggling on at the practice if that's all it's ever going to be — a struggle?'

Her thoughts turned to Rupert once more — his life change wasn't working out so well so using him as a model for change might not be the best idea.

She sighed and stirred herself into action. She was here to feed the other ducks.

Thwarted Hopes

Carrying a cup of pellets Lucy followed the path to the field with the pond. The ducks ran to her as she opened the gate.

This triggered happy memories from her childhood. She'd had responsibility for feeding the chickens.

They stopped a few yards away when they realised it wasn't the usual human. She dropped the cupful of feed into their dog bowl and stepped back.

They dived in and pellets flew everywhere. Lucy smiled at their lack of table manners. It was every duck for herself. The drake supervised, quacking protectively as his girls got stuck in.

As she returned Lucy wandered along the lush and productive vegetable beds. Courgettes were flowering already, the broad beans were showing their first tiny pods, shards of onion leaves looked architectural and stately bouquets of chard stood proudly.

Could she and Jamie have been able

to afford this place if they, along with Tony, hadn't expanded the business?

Perhaps they could have lived here, tending plants and collecting hens' eggs from the nest boxes in the coops every morning, like when she was growing up.

Though had Jamie had wanted that, or was it her dream alone? She remembered it was he who had persuaded her not to look around the place, because they couldn't afford it.

Had he been trying to tell her something, like her father suggested? Had she been blinkered in their relationship, seeing only what she wanted to see?

If his father hadn't died Jamie would still be here . . .

But such thoughts led to a complete dead end. They had taken on that huge loan; Tony did die unexpectedly and, even if he had lived another twenty years, probably Jamie would have admitted his true dreams and aspirations eventually.

It was better to have found out at the beginning of their life together. Had they got married and started a family would

Jamie have stayed, resenting what he'd missed out on?

Or would he still have gone, leaving Lucy feeling obliged to go with him rather than struggle on as a single working mum?

She returned to the car. These thoughts were pointless.

It would be better to sell her share of the surgery and find a job which offered financial security and was not too far away. She could distance herself from this unhappy past without leaving North Millton, after all, surely.

The boot of her Subaru was still open. As she reached up to close it she spotted something white lodged in the junction between the floor and the wing.

She leaned forward and plucked out a feather. It must be from one of the Embden geese she had transported to and from Jack Turner's farm.

There was usually so much stuff in her boot Lucy hadn't noticed it.

Then a vision of Rupert's car on the day she'd helped pack away unsold goods from the stall flashed through her mind.

His boot had been empty apart from a pair of wellies, which she'd moved. The boot lining was dark grey, almost black.

No way would she have missed a white goose feather.

So, if it hadn't been present then, how had the police found it now? How had a feather from stolen goods made its way into Rupert's boot after the geese were recovered?

It made no sense, unless someone who wanted Rupert to seem guilty had planted it. That someone might also have planted the empty quail box and the halter.

An icy feeling spread through her as she worked through the possibilities and kept coming back to the same one.

Yesterday's conversation with her father replayed in her head. Just because she'd known someone a long time didn't mean they wouldn't lie to her.

Jamie lied. Mrs Brookes lied about Paddington. Probably Jack Turner was lying about his horses.

Would it be a surprise if someone she'd known most of her life was lying to her?

She looked at her phone for a long time.

Her father was right. She needed to trust someone and her instincts told her that person was Rupert.

★ ★ ★

After hours of questioning Rupert took a taxi home and hauled his tired limbs from the back seat. As the cab drove off an unlit Longmeadow House loomed at the side of the road like a troll waiting to ambush him.

He shuddered. His new life was becoming a nightmare, with even his home seeming a threat. What else awaited him?

His thoughts turned to the stables and his precious ducks. Would he find more malevolence there?

A tight band squeezing his chest he headed straight for Alison, Gabriel and the others. He opened the fox-proof outer door and the gate that barricaded their stall.

Moonlight showed Alison as a shadow in her nest box. The other ducks lay dotted across the wood shavings like a flotilla of small boats in a sleepy harbour. All safe and sound.

Rupert gulped air and said a silent thank-you to Lucy. Why had he doubted she would look after them?

She wouldn't leave them to the mercy of foxes out of petty mistrust.

Calmer now, his attention returned to Alison. The ducklings were due to hatch any time though that would be a miracle.

Indian runners were notoriously bad mothers and rarely raised young naturally.

Still, Alison hadn't read the books and seemed to be coping perfectly. He hoped she would be rewarded soon with babies.

His guts twisted, as they did every time he thought about children. Ten years ago he still had had that hope ahead of him. But nature had thwarted him and crushed his dreams.

Rupert let himself into his home and

went to bed. Tomorrow was another day. He'd worry about things then.

A Rare Condition

Lucy let herself into the surgery. She wasn't scheduled to work this Sunday but needed to check old records.

She clicked the computer on, logged in and searched for records of Jack Turner's original stallion, the one her dad claimed Tony had treated for lameness.

Eventually she found it. Dr Faustus.

What she read convinced her even more that Uncle Fester's disappearance was fishy.

Tony had attended Dr Faustus, Uncle Fester's grandsire, with lameness. He ruled out causes such as strained ligaments and suspected a neurological condition.

But before he made a firm diagnosis the horse died unexpectedly. Just like Tonto. And now Uncle Fester had disappeared.

No wonder Jack wanted to buy a new horse. His existing bloodline probably had a genetic fault and he was too crooked, or too tight, to find out for sure.

Meanwhile he had been hoping Tony was wrong, or that he'd breed a stallion that was free of the defective gene.

But what had happened to Uncle Fester? And how did this relate to the other thefts?

Was his disappearance a coincidence or had Jack rid himself of a worthless horse?

There must be some way to uncover the truth, though Lucy couldn't see it.

She now understood her attitude must change. People she'd grown up alongside and considered to be honest and hardworking were taking advantage and worse.

Enough was enough. Her father had been right — in some respects she had been a brick wall. It was time to knock down that wall to clear the road ahead.

She e-mailed Elaine, giving her carte blanche to chase outstanding debts and to seek out suitable practitioners to rent the empty treatment room.

Then she locked up and left, determined to see Rupert. She wanted to share her suspicions and hear how the police questioning had gone.

First she drove over to discuss things with her dad. They sat outside and talked.

'You reckon Jack Turner's horses were duffs and he's been covering it up?'

Lucy nodded.

'The value would plummet if his stallions were diagnosed. Jack couldn't wait for Tony to do that. If the trait was dominant it would render his horse useless for breeding purposes because fifty per cent of his offspring would be affected.

'It's a rare condition in thoroughbreds so I guess he figured Tony was wrong or the odds were good enough to get an unaffected stallion from which he could continue to breed.'

'But in subsequent generations the condition was presenting earlier?'

Lucy nodded. Sometimes, as a faulty gene passed down the generations, the afflicted animals were either more badly affected or affected at an earlier age.

Sometimes both.

'I doubt Jack could claim on his insurance if the truth came out.'

'Wouldn't surprise me,' Basil said. 'He's always been a rum 'un, has Jack.'

'But what does this mean?' Lucy asked. 'Has Jack engineered Uncle Fester's disappearance and Tonto's lightning strike?'

Her dad shrugged.

'It's been known. It was common, years back, for certain farmers to fake lightning strikes in animals they wanted rid of.

'Aren't vets wise to that trick now?'

'They should be.' She frowned. 'Maybe that was genuine.'

'Merely fortuitous, you mean.' He nodded.

'So, if Jack Turner faked Uncle Fester's disappearance, was he just taking advantage of the other thefts?'

'If,' her father repeated, his face grave.

'That's a big accusation, Lucy.'

'I know. But it makes sense, doesn't it?'

He hesitated before answering.

'I'm afraid it does. But I doubt we'll ever get proof.'

Lucy tended to agree.

'Still, if he did — and don't forget he had the two stolen geese — is he more deeply involved in these thefts?'

'Lucy, why would he keep animals he'd stolen? That's daft.'

'I know. Unless it's a double bluff! He had a good explanation for how he acquired them via his sister.'

'He could have dropped the halter in Rupert's bin, too, to deflect suspicion. I had questioned him about the disappearances. Maybe he got nervous.'

Her father's expression showed doubt.

'Michael could have planted the halter. Or anyone passing by.'

The more Lucy pondered, the less she understood. Yet, while she might never discover what happened to Jack's horses, she needed to do something about it.

'Whatever you do,' Basil told her, 'always remember I'll be right behind you.'

Yes, he would be. Dad was dependable.

Confronting Michael

On rising that morning Rupert had found a scribbled note from Lucy behind his front door.

Rupert, we need to talk.

Talk about what? The message felt ominous. He half expected her to distance herself, like she had the previous time the police had interviewed him.

Although he had done nothing wrong, mud sticks. Would this be a 'dear John' sort of conversation?

His heart sped up a touch as her car appeared and parked up. A confident, determined-looking Lucy stepped out.

He made an effort to keep his hand steady as he poured coffee from his stove-top Moca machine.

'That smells wonderful,' she told him as she entered through the open kitchen door and casually dropped her keys on the work surface.

'Stirred, not shaken,' Rupert replied with what he hoped was an enigmatic

Bond smile.

'How are you?'

As an opening it was as good as any he had imagined.

Maybe this would turn out OK.

'As well as I can be, I guess.'

He gestured for her to sit.

'I've never been the prime suspect for major theft before so I'm not sure how I should feel. I slept well, if that's any gauge.'

Lucy pulled out a chair and blew on her coffee.

'How did it go at the station? Do they think you did it?'

Rupert shrugged.

'Honestly? I'm still their only suspect and two pieces of hard evidence point to me. They didn't charge me so I take that as a positive.'

'But you didn't do it.'

It was a statement, not a question, and Rupert's heart stuttered for a second. Did she believe him?

He shook his head.

'No, I didn't. My phone logs my movements and I was able to show everywhere I've been for the last three months. It proved I was at home on the nights of the thefts.'

'You could have left your phone behind,' Lucy pointed out.

'That's what they said.' He grimaced.

'The feather they found in your car,' Lucy said after another sip. 'How big was it?'

'Quite big.' Rupert held his two index fingers about six inches apart. 'I'd never seen it before. I'm sure it wasn't in my car when they took it away.'

'The thing is, Rupert . . .'

His mouth went dry. What new bombshell was she about to drop?

'The thing is, I can't remember seeing it in your car, either. And I helped you load it after the farmer's market. That boot was empty except for a pair of wellies.'

Rupert's head swam. He had a witness to his innocence. And it was Lucy!

He let the information sink in then nodded slowly.

Lucy continued.

'So I asked myself, if it wasn't there after the goose thefts how did it suddenly appear after the police had removed your car?'

'Someone planted it?'

'Unless you put it there for a misguided joke, what other explanation is there?

'And I can't think of another reasonable explanation for my box reappearing in your stables. Frankly, Rupert, you're not that stupid!'

He couldn't help himself. He stood and hugged her.

She gasped.

'I'm sorry,' he said and let her go. 'I've been so scared. You won't believe how much hope it gives me to hear you say that.'

'We all need hope,' she replied. 'Especially when we've done nothing wrong.'

'You're right.'

'Someone has got it in for you, it seems, but I'm behind you, Rupert. You don't have to fight this alone.

'I'm only sorry it's taken this, and a few stiff words from my father, to stop me from doubting you. I'm also sorry I turned my back on you before.'

Her words shot the biggest imaginable surge of optimism through his veins. He was floating, his feet swathed in fluffy clouds far off the ground.

He caught her hands in his.

'Thank you. That means such a lot to me.'

She squeezed his hands affectionately.

'I'm just happy I can help, Rupert. So, what will we do next?'

He saw only one option.

'You must tell the police. They'll believe you.'

She nodded and pulled her hands away to reach for her phone.

'I will, I promise. But I want to speak to Michael first. We both should, I think.'

Rupert frowned. He didn't want to speak to the special constable. The man held a big grudge against him.

'Why? He never takes anything I say seriously. Why can't we go straight to the

Bickerston police?'

She held a finger up to silence him as she waited on the call going through, then muttered in frustration when she got no reply.

'He's probably out training.' She tapped a finger to her lips. 'Though he could be in his garden.

'Like you, he has a huge country garden. He inherited it from his parents. He could be there.'

Rupert fidgeted in the passenger seat as Lucy drove.

'You haven't explained why we're doing this.'

'Michael knows more than he's letting on,' she answered. 'I want to confront him about it.'

The set to her jaw told Rupert that, whatever she planned, it wasn't a cosy chat with an old friend.

Ten minutes later they pulled up outside a small, detached, Edwardian brick cottage on a lane he'd never seen before.

The place looked deserted apart from the red Ford Ka he'd seen when Michael had visited him at Longmeadow.

Lucy strode up to the front door and tried the handle. It didn't yield. She knocked.

'Michael?' No answer.

'Round the back,' she ordered and he followed her round the side of the building.

They reached the rear and Lucy rattled the back door.

She stood with her hands on her hips and stared at the upstairs windows.

'Michael!' she yelled.

With Lucy in this mood Rupert thought it was in Michael's interests to be elsewhere. Perhaps he was hiding, after all.

She tapped her toes on York stone flags, her gaze roving over the rear of the house. The only sounds other than her tapping were leaves rustling in the treetops and something cheeping in the shed.

They looked at each other.

'Does he keep birds?' Rupert asked.

'No.'

Lucy was already pulling at the pad-locked door. She peered through the window into the dark interior.

Rupert peered in, too. It might be his imagination but he suspected the shed contained eight Japanese quail.

Jealousy

While they waited for the police to arrive Rupert watched Lucy pace. She had been magnificent on the phone, insisting on them sending someone immediately.

Her father arrived first. Rupert nodded a greeting to the stocky man who he remembered as very jocular.

Basil Pugh wasn't smiling or quipping today. His expression was stern as he shook Rupert's hand and squinted through the small shed window.

'They sound like my birds but I can't rightly see anything. The police won't come out for this, will they, though?'

Lucy looked indignant.

'Of course they will. Stolen goods found in the possession of one of their own? I'm surprised they aren't here already.'

'Lucy was a tour de force on the phone,' Rupert told him. 'They'll come. But I'm not sure me being here helps.'

Lucy stared at him.

'Why?'

'I'm their prime suspect. Won't it look suspicious that I'm here?'

'Rupert, I dragged you here. Trust me.'

Basil muttered something about Lucy being a fine one to talk, but fell silent when she scowled at him.

A few minutes later two officers arrived. Lucy greeted one as Bobby. The second introduced himself as P.C. Shaw.

Lucy explained Michael might have the stolen quail in his shed. They replied they'd need the owner's permission to open it and pointed to the padlock.

'That might take all day,' Lucy argued.

She stepped forward and moved the tumblers on the lock, which opened.

'You knew the number all along?' Rupert asked, shocked.

Lucy shrugged.

'Michael uses the same number for everything. His phone, his iPad. Wouldn't surprise me if it's part of his computer password as well.'

'We should have waited for Michael to

arrive,' PC Shaw said, though he peered into the shed anyway.

'He has a point,' Basil put in. 'They'll be saying you took them and put them in there, Lucy.'

'Thanks, Dad!' She shot him a fierce look.

They all crowded around to peer inside. The shed did contain eight Japanese quail.

'I don't believe it!' Rupert felt his blood pressure rise. 'He stole those birds then blamed it on me!'

'That's a bit premature,' Bobby argued. 'Are these your birds, Mr Pugh?'

'Maybe.' Basil stepped inside the shed. 'They're the right type and number. I didn't know Michael kept quail, did you, Lucy?'

'He never mentioned it,' she answered through clenched teeth. 'I wonder why.'

Rupert shook his head.

'So he stole the birds from my porch and returned the box while I was in the garden with my volunteers! How did he know you were there that afternoon?'

'I have a theory about that,' Lucy began but P.C. Shaw stepped in.

'We can't say anything for certain. Michael must explain the presence of these birds.'

'Good luck with that.'

Lucy pulled out her phone to dial his number one more time. Still no answer.

While the police officers discussed what to do next Michael arrived back on his bike, bright red and drenched in sweat.

The colour drained from his face when he saw everyone next to the open shed door.

'Bobby!' He nodded. 'OK, Jed? What's going on here?'

Lucy stepped forward, her lips a tight line.

'Michael, why do you have Rupert's quail in your shed? You lying —'

Her father caught her arm.

'That's enough, Lucy. Let the police handle this.'

Rupert clenched his fists to stop himself from stepping forward and swinging at the man. That would cause far more problems than it would solve.

'Lucy's right.' Michael sagged on to a low brick wall. 'I took them.'

He looked at her, beseeching.

'I'm sorry, Lucy. I was jealous.'

He glanced up at the officers who, until this moment, had been his colleagues.

'I shouldn't have done it. But when you spent so much time with that incomer . . .' He jerked his head in Rupert's direction.

'I have a name.' Rupert stepped forward.

Basil caught his arm, too, and Michael flicked worried eyes to him, then to Lucy.

'I'm glad it's all out in the open. I stole the quail on impulse, then I was stuck with them.'

'You framed Rupert!' Lucy yelled. 'Someone who has just moved to the area and needed your support. How could you?'

'You must know, Lucy.' His eyes pleaded for understanding. 'I wanted us to be together. I thought it was only a matter of time.

'I gave you space to get over Jamie. I was there for you whenever you needed me. Then he turned up!'

'My name is Rupert,' Rupert growled.

'Michael, you need to come to the station with us,' Bobby said quietly.

'I know.' Michael stood. 'Let me shower first, please.'

'What about the birds?' Basil asked.

The police officers looked puzzled.

'I suppose they're evidence.' They turned to Lucy. 'I presume you'll be pressing charges, Miss Pugh?'

'They're not mine, they're Rupert's.'

The officers swivelled their gaze to him.

'Wait!' Lucy cried. 'We're assuming it's only the quail he stole. What about the other thefts?'

Michael blanched and held up both hands.

'I swear I had nothing to do with those.'

'The goose feather in Rupert's car?' Lucy persisted.

'You should leave any questions to us,' Bobby warned.

Rupert stepped forward.

'Then you ask him why he planted that feather in my car. I have a right to know.'

The officers looked perplexed.

'What feather?'

Michael's shoulders slumped.

'I might as well admit it. My chances of a career with the police are over anyway. Yes, I put the feather there.'

He turned to Jed and Bobby.

'I planted evidence in Rupert Chetwynd's car to make it look like he was the animal thief.'

He turned to Lucy.

'I'm sorry. It was wrong, but I was desperate. I was sure it wouldn't be enough to convict him, I just wanted to plant doubt in your mind so you'd hate him.

'Can you ever forgive me?'

'It's not me who needs to forgive you. It's Rupert.'

Before Rupert could respond Lucy tapped her phone and turned the screen towards Michael.

'What I can't forgive you for is this!'

Michael peered at it.

'What is that?'

'A tracker app. I found it last night when a few things became clear.

'That's how you knew when I was at Longmeadow House, isn't it?'

Michael looked confused.

'Yes, I was tracking you, but you knew about it. A year ago we both set our map apps to share our locations so someone could always find us if we got lost or hurt somewhere remote. Remember?'

Rupert saw Lucy's body language change.

'Oh, yes,' she said with what sounded like relief. 'I do remember now. But . . .'

She fiddled with her phone again and showed it to him.

'You're not sharing your position with me any more.'

'I don't know why.' Michael looked a little desperate. 'Perhaps, when I changed my phone a few months ago, the settings on the app changed. I swear it wasn't deliberate.'

'Yes, but if you didn't install the tracker app, then . . .' Lucy turned to Rupert, her eyes wide.

He put both hands up.

'You don't seriously suspect me? Why would I? And how?'

'You could have accessed my phone that time I crashed on your sof —'

Basil stepped forward.

'It was me.'

Everyone stared at him.

'You, Dad? Why?'

'Because you consider yourself inde-structible, Lucy, not a young woman out alone in the middle of nowhere at night in all weathers. It terrifies me.

'When Jamie was here he knew where you were. After he left I worried about you, OK? I tried talking to you about safety but did you listen?

'If I'd known Michael was tracking you,' he added with a grateful glance at him, 'I wouldn't have done it.'

He turned to face the police officers and gestured to the birds.

'You won't have anywhere to keep

these little cheepers, will you? How about we take them off your hands?'

The two officers looked at each other.

'Works for me,' Jed said.

Bobby shrugged.

'Wait,' Rupert interrupted. There were still matters concerning his guilt to clear up. 'The halter. Did you plant that, too?'

Michael shook his head.

'No. We had an anonymous call saying we'd find something incriminating at Longmeadow. If you aren't the thief then someone else planted that.'

Rupert stared at him in disbelief.

'Two different people were trying to pin the thefts on me?'

Michael nodded miserably.

'I don't know who the other person is.'

'Do you remember anything about the anonymous caller?' Lucy asked.

'Just that it was a woman with a very posh voice.'

Lucy's eyes blazed.

'Jack's sister!'

The Blame Game

'Come on.' Lucy headed back towards the road.

'Where are you going?' Basil asked.

'To confront Jack Turner about his horses,' she called over her shoulder.

'Oh, no, you don't.' Basil moved quickly for an older man with dodgy knees.

He stood in front of his daughter, blocking her way.

'Leave this to the police. Let them find evidence, then question him. It won't help if you go in with all guns blazing.'

'Horses?' Rupert repeated, confused. 'He only lost one, didn't he?'

'It's a long story but we suspect Uncle Fester's disappearance was planned.'

'By Jack?'

Lucy nodded.

Rupert blinked. She hadn't been kidding when she'd said they needed to talk!

He just wished they'd done it before this showdown, when he might have been able to absorb everything. As it was his head was spinning.

'We can't stand here all day,' Basil said. 'We need to round up those birds.'

The three of them set about catching eight small and nimble birds who did not wish to be caught. For Rupert it was an excellent antidote to the previous half hour.

Eventually the quail were safe in Lucy's animal carrier and Michael had left with Jed and Bobby.

'Shall I put them in your car?' Lucy asked.

'Certainly not. They were a present for your young man. I just hope he looks after them better this time.' Basil winked at Rupert.

Lucy blushed.

'He's not my —'

'Anyway, must be going. Things to do.' Basil left so fast that Rupert guessed he wanted to leave the two of them together.

'I'm sorry.' Lucy avoided eye contact as she loaded the carrier into her boot. 'I have no idea why he thinks we're together. I haven't said anything to give him that impression.'

Rupert tried for humour.

'Wishful thinking? Perhaps he wants a son-in-law with a smallholding so he can talk about farming.'

They got into her car.

'Your place?'

Rupert nodded.

'I need coffee. Actually what I need is a stiff gin, but I'm going to have coffee.'

'Me, too,' Lucy agreed as she pulled away down the lane.

'I need to construct a temporary home for the quail. We can't leave them in the carry box.'

'I'm happy to help with that,' Lucy said. 'Hard work will help take my mind off this, this mess.'

Rupert decided 'mess' was the most understated word imaginable.

'I can't take it all in,' he admitted. 'Tell me about Michael and Jack Turner. We probably need to talk about us, too.'

Lucy glanced at him.

'Why? We're not even dating.'

'No, but we could be, don't you think?'
Lucy nodded.

'I've been reluctant to get involved because of Jamie. I sense you have, too.'

'More than reluctant, Lucy. I don't want to be the next man to let you down.'

She kept her eyes fixed straight ahead.

'That sounds ominous. You're not a mass murderer, are you?'

'No.' Rupert clenched his fists as he thought about Michael and Jack. 'Though I might make an exception for some of my neighbours!'

Lucy laughed lightly.

'Try not to think too harshly of Michael, if you can.'

'Why? He wanted me behind bars!'

'No, he just wanted you out of the way. It's inexcusable, but I blame myself.'

She sighed.

'I could have avoided all this.'

'How?'

'I suspected he was in love with me but, as usual, I avoided doing anything about it. I kept my blinkers on.

'I've done the same with Elaine, not

letting her get on with what needs doing just because it didn't fit my vision.

'Looking back, I may have done the same with Jamie,' she added.

Rupert hoped she wasn't about to blame herself for another person's wrongdoing.

'What do you mean as regards Michael?'

'If I had told him I could never return his feelings then he might not have been driven to such desperate measures.'

Rupert ran his hand through his hair.

'His actions were not normal, Lucy. I'm so mad that I can't even think about what he did.'

'Rightly so, but you're in the clear now.'

There was that.

'Why do you think you did something wrong with Jamie?' he asked, to steer his thoughts away from the anger still surging through him.

She sighed.

'It was something my dad said the other day, about how keen Tony and I had been on Jamie and me joining the partnership.

'Looking back, I know Jamie was always fascinated by exotic animals. He suggested spreading our wings a little — working in other practices in other areas — before we settled down.

'I wouldn't hear of it. All I ever wanted to do was work here.'

She frowned.

'Also, he wouldn't discuss taking on anywhere as expensive as Longmeadow because he didn't want to load himself up with all that debt.'

With the car stopped at a junction, Lucy looked at Rupert.

'He urged caution with the surgery extension, too. I think, now, he didn't want to tie himself down to North Millton. I just didn't see it then.'

He rested his hand on her arm.

'These things are always clearer in hindsight, Lucy. The important thing is you learn the lesson and take that forward.'

She nodded and pulled off again.

'I didn't tell you the news Jamie's mum shared with me the other day, did I?'

'No. What?'

'He's seeing a marine biologist and they're expecting a baby.'

'Oh.' He was unsure how Lucy expected him to respond to this. 'How does that make you feel?'

She shrugged.

'OK, I guess. I'm glad he's happy, really I am. But it's another clue I should have noticed. He was always talking about starting a family. How one of us would need to reduce our work hours and what would that do to the finances?'

'And how about you?'

Rupert held his breath. Here was the question he'd wanted to ask but had so far considered inappropriate.

'Me? Oh, I figured we'd start with a dog, then a few chickens and, if we had space, a goat or some pot-bellied pigs.'

Lucy glanced at him nervously.

'A pig or two would fit perfectly in the end stall of your stables, don't you think?'

Rupert grinned with relief. Maybe this wasn't a problem, after all. Now was his chance to find out once and for all.

'You were planning a menagerie, not a family, then.'

She pulled the car to a stop.

'We're here. And those birds are cheeping to get out. Let's get them sorted, shall we?'

A New Family

It took two hours to make the stall next to the ducks quailproof. Rupert couldn't allow the new birds to roam free in his fields as they'd escape and not come back.

As quail can fly, unlike ducks, Rupert and Lucy also had to roof the stall.

Finally, he spread straw on the floor and, at Lucy's insistence, found some logs and branches to give the nervous birds somewhere to hide if they felt threatened.

Lucy brought the cage and opened the door. She and Rupert watched for a few minutes as the tiny birds darted about the wood shavings, investigated the twigs and found their way into all the corners of their new home.

'I'll fix up something better tomorrow,' Rupert said as they took a last look. 'They need access to fresh air and sunlight.'

Lucy stilled.

'Can you hear a peeping noise?'

'Like a car horn?'

'No. Like ducklings.' Lucy dashed to the duck stall. 'Look! Alison has her babies!'

'What?' Rupert strode over.

Alison was off her nest, drinking from the water bowl. Behind her six perfect, multi-coloured ducklings with triangular black feet scurried through the straw, peeping.

Rupert grinned like an idiot as he caught Lucy in a hug and whirled her around.

'Isn't that the most wonderful thing?'

'Easy, tiger.' Lucy eased away as they stopped spinning. 'I take it you're happy?'

'Beyond happy. Do you know how rarely Indian runner ducks successfully hatch their own ducklings?'

'I am a vet, remember. You're right. It's a minor miracle. Alison is an exceptional duck, with an exceptional owner.'

The grin on his face tugged at something deep inside her. He deserved this after all he'd been subjected to recently.

On impulse she stood on tiptoe and kissed his cheek.

'You must be a great dad, Rupert.'

She saw pain flit across his face before he caught himself.

Lucy stepped back.

'I'm sorry, it was thoughtless to say that. You wanted children, didn't you?'

Rupert nodded.

'Still, what will be will be. We never had that coffee, did we? Though I guess champagne is more in order now.'

Lucy ignored the fact that he'd tried to change the subject. This was important.

She realised now that he'd tried to talk about her thoughts about children in the car. As usual, she'd failed to pick up on it.

'Is that why you think you'll let me down?' she asked.

Again a nod.

'You said you and Jamie were going to settle down and start a family. You won't ever be able to do that with me.'

Lucy stared at him.

'When did I say that?'

'Over dinner, after you helped me at the stall.'

She cast her mind back. She couldn't remember saying those words but it sounded reasonable.

Jamie had wanted children and she'd gone along with the idea in theory. But had she meant it?

She looped her arm through Rupert's.

'Let's get that drink, shall we?'

Soon they were sitting at his picnic table sipping elderflower cordial, which seemed better suited than coffee or bubbly to quench the thirst they'd worked up.

'So you don't want children?' Rupert asked. 'It's important, Lucy. I'm falling for you and I sense you're attracted to me, too.

'But we shouldn't become involved if we know this thing could ultimately come between us. We'll both get hurt again.'

'I don't know,' she answered honestly. 'I was — am — too busy enjoying my job to consider children. Besides, where would I fit childcare? Between evening surgery and night visits?'

'Your views might change.'

'They might, but couldn't we base a relationship on having a fulfilling life together, just us and a bunch of animals?'

'What if you get broody in the future?'

He was almost holding his breath in anticipation of the answer. His whole future seemed to hang on it.

'There are other options. There must be plenty of children who need a loving home, complete with ducks and runner beans.'

Could this be true? Was he dreaming? Was Lucy saying what he wanted to hear, not what she felt?

If it were a dream it wouldn't matter if he kissed her.

He took Lucy's face in his hands, cradling it as he would one of Alison's babies, and touched his lips to hers.

Her whole body softened and wilted against his as though all her tension was ebbing away.

Encouraged, he folded her into his arms and kissed her properly.

Changed Days

Having finished seeing patients, Lucy took a deep breath and smiled. Yesterday she had discovered Michael had been lying and stealing and she and Rupert had spent the afternoon kissing, talking and drinking cordial at Longmeadow House.

Today was the first day of the rest of her new life. For once she wasn't exhausted. She was elated. Everything was going to be just fine.

She rose and walked into Elaine's office, pausing to make two herb teas on the way.

'Did you get my e-mail?' she asked, placing one cup in front of her manager.

Elaine looked up.

'Yes. I hope you meant it, because I sent out ten final notices this morning!'

'Good.' Lucy pulled up a chair and sat down. 'Dad says you have some excellent ideas for expanding the workforce.'

Elaine stared at her for a few seconds.

'Are you all right?'

'Never better. Look!' Lucy pointed to her face. 'No bags under my eyes.'

'Right, well . . .' Elaine turned to the computer. 'If you're serious, we received some enquiries from nurses with advanced qualifications. I spoke to our current staff. They agree that if we employed one of them she could take over a chunk of your current workload.

'That would allow you to concentrate on the tasks only a vet can do. I've built a business case.'

The printer whirred into life and shortly Lucy held a very professional but mercifully brief document in her hand.

She flicked through it.

'Thank you, this makes perfect sense. Set up some interviews. By the way, I'm moving in with my dad.'

Elaine's mouth fell open.

'It's an obvious solution to my cash flow problem. I was too obstinate to acknowledge it before, but I only had one enquiry from a potential lodger who needed a room short term.'

Elaine's eyebrows rose.

'Lodger?'

Lucy suppressed a giggle.

'However, a friend of a friend knows a lovely young couple with a baby who want to rent the whole house. They paid a deposit of three months' rent!'

That would wipe out her overdraft when it cleared. And the monthly rent cheque would cover future mortgage payments.

'I'm, um, pleased for you,' Elaine said, though Lucy saw she was flabbergasted.

'Did you hear about Michael?'

Lucy was aware most of the village would be gossiping about it. She might as well get it out into the open rather than endure whispers behind her back.

'Is it true he was stalking you?'

'Not exactly.'

Lucy explained how she had shared her location with him for safety reasons.

'But he kept appearing in the same place as you.'

'Only at Rupert's,' Lucy said. 'He was jealous.'

Elaine nodded.

'I'm not surprised. He was dotty about you. It must have been hard when a handsome rival appeared.'

Lucy sighed.

'I know. I can't help feeling sorry for him. He shouldn't have done what he did but he's lost everything. His job, a chance of working for the police . . .'

'And the love of his life,' Elaine added.

'At least Rupert has agreed not to press charges against him. The police will probably charge him for planting evidence.'

'Will he go to jail?'

'It seems likely. But he's admitted everything and hopefully his sentence will be minimal. He's well-liked in the community so with any luck he'll get straight back on his feet.

Elaine nodded.

'It seems harsh but he shouldn't have done it. So, what's happening about Jack Turner?'

'How do you know about him?' Lucy asked, surprised.

Elaine gave her one of those 'This is North Millton' looks. Of course, the local rumour mill would have been in overdrive this last 24 hours.

'I'm sure it was his sister, Loretta, who made the anonymous phone call about the halter in Rupert's bin. Presumably Jack planted it.'

'Loretta?' Elaine looked surprised. 'She phoned from New Zealand?'

'No. She lives in Lancaster.'

Elaine shook her head.

'Who told you that?'

'Jack did,' Lucy replied, her ears pricking up. 'He phoned her and I spoke to her. Didn't I?'

'Doubtful. I'm friends with her on social media and she emigrated from Lancaster to New Zealand two years ago. Why would Jack lie about something like that?'

Lucy shared her theory that Jack might be using the thefts to claim the money for his horses who had a genetic defect.

'You must tell the police about Loretta,' she urged. 'They took his trailer away to be examined. This is another piece of crucial evidence.'

'I will, after I've banked Jack's cheque.' Elaine grinned and waved a piece of paper in the air.

Lucy stared at it.

'He paid?'

'In full. Let's hope it doesn't bounce!'

'Oh, Elaine, things really are looking up, aren't they?'

'We'll be fine, Lucy, thanks to you. Which reminds me.'

She pushed a leaflet across her desk.

Lucy turned it around and read the title.

Pet Massage Therapy.

'She's searching for a room to rent,' Elaine explained.

Lucy laughed and pushed the leaflet back.

'Ask her in for a chat.' She picked up her cup and rose. 'Well, I'm off.'

'Going anywhere nice?' Elaine asked much too innocently.

Lucy rolled her eyes. Word travelled fast.

'I have a visit.'

'Will you be picking up a sandwich from Josie's?' Elaine probed. 'To eat at your desk?'

Clearly she suspected Lucy had other plans.

Which she did.

In the house of her dreams Rupert promised cheese, pickles and salad on sourdough, a play with the ducklings and lots more of those delicious kisses.

Bliss!

We do hope that you have enjoyed reading this large print book.

Did you know that all of our titles are available for purchase?

We publish a wide range of high quality large print books including:
Romances, Mysteries, Classics
General Fiction
Non Fiction and Westerns

Special interest titles available in large print are:
The Little Oxford Dictionary
Music Book, Song Book
Hymn Book, Service Book

Also available from us courtesy of Oxford University Press:
Young Readers' Dictionary
(large print edition)
Young Readers' Thesaurus
(large print edition)

For further information or a free brochure, please contact us at:
Ulverscroft Large Print Books Ltd.,
The Green, Bradgate Road, Anstey,
Leicester, LE7 7FU, England.
Tel: (00 44) **0116 236 4325**
Fax: (00 44) **0116 234 0205**

Other titles in the
Linford Romance Library:

LIGHTS, CAMERA, ACTION!

Wendy Janes

Along with five other couples, cash-strapped Hayley and Craig are flown to a romantic island paradise as contestants in a new upmarket TV programme: Britain's Most Romantic Couple. There's a £100,000 prize up for grabs for the winners.

Relationships are put under the spotlight, and friendships and rivalries emerge, as the couples attempt entertaining creative, physical and practical tasks.

Will Hayley and Craig show they deserve to be crowned Britain's Most Romantic Couple?

A RISK WORTH TAKING

Alyson Hilbourne

Meg and her father run a public house by the sea, but Pa is also involved in the 'night business' — helping the smugglers evade the excise men. More than anything, Meg wishes he could get out of the gang's clutches; but when Pa brings home an injured man to hide in their attic, it seems the family will be more involved than ever . . .

NUMBER ONE FAN

Debbie Chase

Ordinary Yorkshire girl Angie-Marie gets the break of a lifetime and becomes international pop sensation Anya Starr. But the path to stardom is never a smooth one, and Anya soon realises that not everyone is what they seem . . .

MOON HALL MYSTERY

Margaret Mounsdon

Millie Midwinter thought she had found her dream job when Charlie Pendennis made her an offer of employment with a manor house thrown in. It was the perfect solution to her current personal crisis — or was it? Charlie's sister Becky had gone missing, and there were rumours of strange goings-on down in the cove. It wasn't long before Millie began to wonder if she had made a serious error of judgement.

Other titles in the
Linford Romance Library:

LOVE'S DECEPTION

Wendy Kremer

After Kitty's gran died, she went to visit her godmother Isabel, her gran's best friend. Intending only to deliver a keepsake, she ended up staying. There she met Isabel's grandson James, who was rich and successful — and highly suspicious of her. He rubbed her up the wrong way from the very start. Would they ever learn to like each other?